TIME OF DEATH

A TIME TRAVEL DETECTIVE MYSTERY

NATHAN VAN COOPS

Skylighter
Press

For Grandma Maggie, who loves mysteries.
Sorry for the swear words.

Get a free time travel novella when you join the newsletter for books by Nathan Van Coops. Get your free book here:

https://dl.bookfunnel.com/997t8zzj7o

1

_____

The padlock snapped open with a satisfying click.

I scooped the stopwatch from my desk and checked the time. "And that's a new record."

I lobbed the lock into the cardboard box near the door, and it clattered among the dozen others. "Better step up your game, Waldo. I'm getting too good for you." I flourished my favorite lock pick, gave it a kiss for luck, then slid it back into my shirt pocket.

My office was empty. Rain assaulted the southern-facing windows that looked out over Central Avenue. Cars and pedestrians dashed about their business outside, but Waldo remained silent. Likely because his settings hadn't picked up on a request for action. That or my A.I. assistant was becoming a poor loser.

"You could at least offer a 'well done' or something," I said, rising from my swivel chair and stretching before picking up the roll of packing tape. "That was at least six more than they sent in the last box."

"Congratulations, sir." The deep voice came from the speaker embedded in the desk lamp. "You have once again proven yourself more intelligent than inanimate lumps of steel."

Attitude. Always the attitude.

"Your sarcasm is noted, Waldo. Print a return label for this, will you?" I ran packing tape across the box and placed it near the hallway door for the mail carrier to retrieve.

The freelance lock-picking service was only a side hobby, but it kept my skills sharp, and every package that went out carried a handful of my business cards. Greyson Travers. Private Investigator.

"Your eleven o'clock appointment has arrived."

Waldo's announcement was accompanied by footfalls on the stairs. I kicked the box of locks till it sat neatly in the corner and rolled the sleeves of my Oxford shirt another rotation up my forearms. I quickly crossed my customer lobby that consisted of only four chairs, a coffee table, and a ficus, then opened the main hallway door.

The woman in the hallway froze, her fist arrested mid knock. Anyone else would've looked ridiculous. She didn't.

"Mrs. Phillips," I said.

Isla Phillips had sounded older on the phone, but the conversation had been brief. The woman standing before me was only in her late twenties, dressed like she'd stepped directly from an Anthropologie dressing room. Her skin tone suggested a heritage that was at least biracial. Part angel perhaps. Her embroidered blue mini dress featured flowing full-length sleeves and a V neck that bordered on plunging. A delicate gold pendant hung between well-defined collar bones. Everything south of that was worth observation as well, but her daintily freckled nose and stunning hazel eyes held me hostage.

That and I'm a gentleman.

"Mr. Travers?"

"Greyson. Please come in." I took her dripping umbrella, then gestured toward my open office door.

She walked through to my office, and the place instantly

smelled like wildflowers and summertime. I felt like turning a cartwheel.

Isla Phillips paused near the two pine-and-steel guest chairs opposite my desk. "You keep a very tidy office."

"Cluttered room, cluttered mind," I said, moving around the desk and waiting for her to sit. She chose the right-hand guest chair and sank gracefully to the seat before crossing her legs. I only had time to admire her well-defined calves before fixing her with my brightest how-can-I-save-your-day smile. I sat and folded my hands across my lap.

"I've never hired a private detective before," she began. "But I thought it would be best to explain my situation in person."

"Phones are the worst," I said. "I'm happy you came to the fun side of the bridge. Can I offer you a drink?" I gestured toward the stainless steel mini fridge built into the credenza. "I have a variety of craft beers. All of Tampa Bay's finest. Coffee, et cetera."

"No, thank you." She studied my face. "You're younger than I imagined. I don't know why, but I thought you'd be . . ."

"Less hip with the kids?" I offered.

"More . . . traditional," she replied.

"I can put out the scotch and ashtrays if it makes you feel more comfortable. Perhaps refer to you as a dame when you leave?"

She gave me a wan smile and fidgeted with her wedding band. The diamond at the center of the engagement ring could capsize a small boat.

"I suppose I ought to tell you about my husband."

"Hmm. Mr. Phillips," I said, to astound her with my detective skills.

"It's going on six months since the police closed the investigation and ruled his death a suicide. They tell me they'll consider reopening it if I come up with new information they find plausible, but I haven't found anything they say counts. I think the detective I've been talking to has only been humoring me this long because he likes looking at my legs. The last time I called, he tried to ask me out."

"You've come to the right place. I'm immune to beautiful women and their legs."

Isla Phillips eyed me skeptically, ignoring the implied compliment.

"I believe my husband was murdered, Mr. Travers. And I need you to prove it for me."

"Why are the police convinced the case is closed?" I asked.

She sighed. "There was a note. It's in his handwriting, and there were no other fingerprints on the gun except his. But I know they're missing something."

"You want your own detective."

"I've already waited too long for answers from the police. I asked around. They say you can solve any case in days. Are you really that good?"

"I'm at least average. You found me by referral?"

"One of the girls at my work. Said you got her out of a jam. Swears you're the best detective in town."

"Depends on the case. I only take the ones I'm a good fit for."

"Think you're fit to handle mine? Or is your reputation overstated?"

A challenge.

I scratched my fingertips across the ten days of stubble on my jaw. "You ever see The Maltese Falcon? Old black-and-white movie with Humphrey Bogart?"

"No."

"It's a bit of a classic in my field. I can admit I'm every bit as good as Miles Archer." I pulled my favorite lock pick from my pocket and fidgeted with it, attempting to roll it finger-to-finger one-handed like a coin.

"You do look like you could star in an old movie. You have that kind of face. Sort of striking."

My lock pick escaped my grasp and ended up on the floor.

Utter betrayal.

I rolled my chair closer to the desk so I had something to rest my movie star elbows on. "What makes you think your husband didn't kill himself, Mrs. Phillips?"

Isla Phillips chewed her cheek, then exhaled. "It wouldn't be like him. He wasn't depressed. He was ... determined."

"You don't think it's possible he was hiding a mental illness of some kind?"

"I would've known."

"Financial trouble? Change in his career? Marital issues?"

"We had our difficulties same as anyone, but I know there was nothing that would've made him want to end his life. If anything, he had more to live for."

"Did he have any enemies? People who wished him harm?"

"Not that I know about. But there was another thing. A while ago, someone broke into our house but didn't steal anything. I can't help thinking it was somehow related."

"This was before or after he died?"

"After," Isla said. "And I know it doesn't make sense to think the break-in was connected if he was already dead, but I just can't shake it. I don't know what else to tell you beyond what I've already told the police. And they don't believe me. But I know there's more, and until I find it, I'm not—" She choked up and covered her quivering lower lip with her hand. The composure she had maintained so gracefully was gone and she was suddenly fragile. I resisted the compulsion to reach for her hand. A moment later she collected herself. "I'm not going to give up." She fixed me with her iridescent eyes, now glittering with tears.

It was a convincing show but I didn't buy it. Not yet.

"What aren't you telling me?"

She blinked. Wary.

"There's something else. Or you wouldn't have come to me.

You want a private cop. That means I work for you, not the police. You can spill it."

She bit her lip. Opened her mouth, paused, then finally let it out. "Foster had a record. He was trying to go straight. He had gone straight mostly. But before he died he said he was into something big. Something that would change things for us. He wouldn't tell me what it was and I never found out, but I had the feeling it may have been something illegal. I didn't want to tell the police about it. I knew they'd think it was only more proof he was troubled."

There it was. The real story. Her side anyway.

"My usual turn around is seventy-two hours," I said, and pushed my card across the table. "Fee's listed on the back. Half now, half when I finish. If I run into any unusual expenses I'll clear them with you first. Expect that I'll check in with updates, but don't worry if you can't reach me. I'm on the case."

"You don't want to ask more about him?"

"I do. But first I like to get paid."

Isla picked up the card, wiped at her eyes, and reached for her purse. "This seems expensive. What happens if you don't solve it in seventy-two hours?"

"You can have your money back," I said. "But I'll get you an answer. I can't promise you'll like it, but if you meet me in this office Monday at . . ." I checked the clock, " . . . eleven, you'll have the truth."

The widow pulled a credit card from her wallet, but paused. "Why seventy-two hours? Aren't all cases different?"

"I tried twenty-four but people assumed I was cutting corners."

She blinked again, then rose from her chair to hand her card across the desk. I stood as well.

"You're a very unusual man, Mr. Travers."

I took the card and swiped it over the hidden pay port built into my desk, then handed it back.

"I'm going to do some preliminary research, then I'll contact you with my questions. Can I see you to your car?"

"I'll be fine. Thank you."

I moved around the desk and crossed to the door, opening it for her and retrieving her umbrella. She tucked her wallet back into her purse and paused in the doorway. "When should I expect to hear from you?"

"Will you be home tonight?"

"Yes. I can text you the address."

"I'll stop by."

Isla Phillips took her umbrella as she stepped into the hall, still smelling like summer. I watched her go. At the corner of the stairs, she glanced back and gave me a faint smile. I tried not to melt.

I closed the door and walked back to my desk. "Waldo, get me everything you have on Foster Phillips and put it in my cloud, will you?"

Waldo's voice emanated from the speaker in the lamp again. "The character of Miles Archer died within the first ten minutes of the film version of *The Maltese Falcon*. In the novel, it's in chapter two. Is there something about this case you're not telling me?"

"I like to set a low bar for myself. Feels good later when I'm extra awesome." I tapped a sequence on the surface of my desk with my fingertips and a hidden drawer popped out, revealing a semi-automatic pistol and a watch-like device with a variety of concentric rings on the face.

"You could try allowing yourself more time for once," Waldo offered. "Like a regular private investigator."

I slid the watch-like device onto my wrist and adjusted the dials. "What fun would that be? You know time is never the issue. I can cheat that. Double-check my coordinates for me?"

"Your settings are perfect, as usual."

"Lock the place up for me."

"Have a good trip, sir."

I touched my index finger to the pistol in the drawer, pressed the activation pin on the watch with my other hand, and vanished.

2

I'm a time traveler.

That's what the clients don't know.

Tried telling one once but it was nothing but "I don't believe you. How this, what about that, and why don't you play the stock market?" Boring.

It's just another skill.

Get a job, go to the past, discover the truth, get paid.

Easy.

My hand was still on the gun. Same gun, different place. Ten minutes in the future and two miles across town. My safe room.

Travel by personal wormhole is handy like that.

I took the pistol from its anchor stand and dumped it in the outgoing items bin near the door, then used my fingerprint on the exit lock. The system beeped, logging the time. I stepped outside.

The hexagonal pavers underfoot were dry but the air smelled like rain. The rumble of thunder threatened from downtown.

Hawk, a gargantuan black cat with a tattered right ear, stared at me from the deteriorating wall that encircled the patio. He gave me a slow blink.

"Good to see you too, buddy."

The cat's ears flicked and he raised his eyes to the second story.

Something was up.

There were still a few seconds left on my exit window from the jump room. I opened the door again and snatched my pistol from the bin before the time lock on the door could set. The 9mm Stinger 1911 unlocked in my hand, triggered by a combination of the palm print sensor in the grip and the titanium band on my right ring finger. I kept my index finger on the trigger guard and ascended the steps to my second story garage apartment.

No signs of forced entry. I tried the door and found it unlocked. Not how I left it.

My gun was up as I stepped inside. I scanned the open living area. Kitchen was clear. A sound came from the hallway to the bedrooms. Water running. The sink.

Burglars and hitmen don't usually pause to wash up before a crime.

The bathroom door opened and a tall, middle-aged man wearing shorts and flip flops stepped into the hall.

I lowered my gun. "Shit, Dad. B and E is a good way to get yourself shot."

Benjamin Travers stared back at me. "I didn't B anything. Just needed to wash the blood off. Your ugly cat mauled me." He held up his forearm and displayed several red scratches that were already turning to angry welts. He also had a chronometer on his wrist.

"Hawk is handsome. All the girl cats love him. What are you doing here?"

"Your mother is a persistent worrier."

"I'll visit eventually." I walked to the fridge, pulled two beers out and handed one to my dad.

He walked around the living room while he sipped his, studied the blinds. "How long have you lived here and you still don't have curtains? You bring girls up to this? If anything you should decorate for them."

"I go to your place and insult your aesthetic?" I sank onto the couch with my beer.

"An aesthetic requires some measure of beauty. Like art. Or at least objects that could be deemed artistic. You have blank walls and a doormat." He took a seat next to me.

"I like things simple. What do you care?"

"I just don't get why you want to live in this neighborhood. It's depressing. The decade. All of it. Your mother and I went to a lot of effort trying to raise you somewhere nicer. Better. I don't get why you came back here."

"You used to live in this decade."

"Before I had a choice."

"You said the first rule of time travel is to not make anything worse."

"You thought that meant go live in some armpit of a timeline? Who did they elect as . . . you know what? I'll stop. You gotta live your life." He drank more beer. "How old are you these days? Thirty?"

"I don't know. In my prime, obviously."

"Your mother said to remind you there's a place for you in our time whenever you want it. You could find a job that isn't chasing people's misdeeds all night. Work some regular hours. Maybe see if you remember what the sun looks like."

"Yellow, burny, sky thing. I've seen it. Besides, I like it here. It's where my cat lives."

"A cat isn't a family."

"Maybe I prefer caring for something that stays where I left it. Doesn't expect me to do anything but show up with Meow Mix. Doesn't expect me to be a guy I'm not."

Dad swallowed hard. "I know you didn't ask to be born a time traveler. Didn't ask for the problems that come with it. We did the best we could."

"I'm good. Don't beat yourself up. You bring the car?"

He sighed. "Yeah. I'll drop it by later. You want it in the garage?"

"Leave it out front. I'll handle putting it away."

"Still don't know how you pulled it off."

"You're the one who taught me poker. You really ought to blame yourself."

"Your mom doesn't know I saw you that night."

"Who am I going to tell?"

He got off the couch and put his beer can in the sink. When he came back, I stood and he put a hand on my shoulder. "Take care of yourself, all right? Maybe make some friends or something."

"I've got Waldo. And Hawk. I'm already over-scheduled."

He went to the door. "I'll drop the car by tomorrow."

"Tell Mom not to worry. I'm fine."

"Sure. And I'll tell this sky not to burst." He gave me a wave and shut the door. A moment later, lightning flashed across the sky. Storm was settling in.

Good time to get back to work.

It took me several stops, cross-referencing safe jump locations with Waldo, but I got myself to Hyde Park, a trendy neighborhood of South Tampa in the twilight hours of October 20th, 2018.

The night Foster Phillips died.

The evening was cool and the moon was rising. I stuffed my hands in the pockets of my jeans and whistled as I strolled through Hyde Park Village—an attractive, high-end shopping district filled with attractive high-end people. No one can suspect you of being a time traveler if they are too stunned by your whistling prowess.

I'm the Michael Phelps of whistling.

After doing my best not to ogle a group of fit thirty-something women exiting LuluLemon, I turned down a side street, cruising the sidewalk in front of beautified Old Florida bungalows with wooden porch swings and lawns of verdant St. Augustine grass.

The slice of Americana where Foster and Isla Phillips lived had an oak tree in the front yard and a garage apartment in the back. The porch swing was green and the front door was sunshine yellow. I strolled by slowly, then crossed the street, pulling my wallet out at the corner before circling back. I slipped a business-card-sized sheet from my wallet and punched out one of my eight micro-cameras. They resembled the googly eyes kids stick on kindergarten craft supplies to give them personalities. My cameras were similarly adhesive and I stuck one to the pole of a NO PARKING sign opposite the Phillips' residence. A tree a dozen yards down got one too.

Lurking in a car on stakeouts for hours is an honored tradition of the private investigator trade, but the Impossible Burger with extra guac I'd had for lunch was already sending me toward a siesta. I figured I'd make this quick.

I made a lap of the block and cruised down the alley to check the rear access, depositing another two micro-cameras. I checked my phone to make sure all of the cameras were transmitting, then browsed through a few mugshots Waldo had found of Foster Phillips.

The police department isn't known for flattering photography but Foster presented as a handsome man in his late twenties. He had a sharp, eager face. Isla had described him as determined. I could see it in his eyes. He'd been arrested a few times. Car theft and attempted robbery. Did a couple years but was paroled early for good behavior. Employed by some kind of security firm but had been let go six months ago.

It was on my return lap from the back alley that I spotted the truck. The Mercedes Benz G-Class SUV was black on black from its window tint to the color of its rims. It was parked on a side street but had a clear view of the Phillips' house. The engine was idling and a steady drip of condensation had created a puddle beneath the air conditioning system. Attempting to see inside was like staring into the nothing.

Hyde Park was a nice neighborhood, and it was home to plenty of money-savvy millennials, and probably a few of their parents, but not Russian mafia. Even a half-decade-old G-Class SUV was an eighty-thousand dollar ride. On a woke street full of Mini-Coopers and Priuses, it stuck out like a Mercedes G-Class SUV.

This was one downside to getting around by time travel. I didn't have my own lurker mobile around a corner with which to surveil the suspicious SUV. But I did have my sparkling personality. I tugged my sunglasses from the collar of my shirt and slipped them on, pressing the record button on the in-frame camera, then jaywalked across the street to the driver's side of the Mercedes. I rapped on the window and gave my reflection a winning grin.

I rested my hand on the side-view mirror. The window came down halfway.

"The fuck you want?"

The driver of the car wore sunglasses too, but not as cool as mine. Obviously jealous. He was a hulk of man whose shaved head and abundant neck folds meant he probably didn't have my outstanding hair genes or low cholesterol numbers. A second man was in the passenger seat. He had excellent hair but a pinched, constipated tension to his features. He might be able to compete on the cholesterol front but I doubted Isla Phillips had ever told him he had classic movie star appeal.

"Excuse me, gents. You happen to see a little dog run by? It's a shepherd-yorkie-schnoodle-chow. Goes by Barkley."

"We look like dog catchers to you? Get lost."

The window went back up.

"I'm just gonna keep looking around then!" I shouted to the

closed window. I gave my reflection a wave, then wandered back past the Phillips' house, periodically calling for my dog who stubbornly refused to exist.

My hunt for Barkley was so intense that I almost missed the dented Volkswagen Golf that cruised by. But the driver's face caught my attention. The car swung into the narrow driveway and pulled alongside the bungalow with the yellow door. The engine cut off and the brake lights went out.

Foster Phillips had arrived home.

I was around the corner and out of sight by the time the man climbed out of his car. I pulled my shades off and watched the action with my phone via the micro-cameras. Foster Phillips wore jeans and a Tampa Bay Lightning jersey. He carried a shoulder bag—the kind used for hauling a laptop—and some kind of hard-sided crate, size of a suitcase. He hurried up the steps, ignored his full mailbox, and went directly inside. I toggled between cameras and made sure each was recording.

Whatever happened from here had already happened. It wasn't my job to stop it. But the circumstances did have me curious. I lingered in the alley midway down the block, watching the clock. Took about twenty minutes. I was close enough to hear the gunshot when it went off.

I watched for fifteen more minutes—till the second car pulled into the driveway. Isla Phillips. She took her time getting out of the white Volvo, checked something on her phone, then gathered the mail. Not the actions of a woman who knew she'd find her husband dead in their home.

She entered the front door and disappeared.

No one else came in or out of the Phillips' house. I rewound the recordings and double-checked. Nobody but Isla.

Evidence said suicide.

The camera I'd surreptitiously stuck to the Mercedes' side-view mirror had shown no movement, but now the vehicle started rolling. They passed a police cruiser on its way in. The video feed only lasted another half block before it was out of range. That camera disconnected from my screen.

"Where did you make your fun friends, Foster Phillips?"

I pocketed my phone and took the long way back to Hyde Park Village.

The trip had given me answers, but now I had more questions.

3

As a private detective, my relationship with local police was sometimes frosty. It might get to room temp on a good week. But it was frigid on a bad one. Mostly because I rarely dealt with them face-to-face. Navigating labyrinthian phone directories or filling out online request forms for public records brought out my most colorful swearing. Thankfully, Waldo remained nonplussed. My A.I. assistant kept me at arms length from the local LEOs, but sometimes an in-person meetup had its benefits.

Browsing the public records on the death of Foster Phillips, I discovered the lead detective on the case was someone I knew. And I knew where to find him.

Dave Walsh had aggressively climbed the ranks of the department to become a homicide detective. He played men's league softball when he wasn't on duty and drank after the Wednesday night games at a pseudo-Irish bar called MacDinton's. I found him there with a few of the guys from his team drinking Miller Lite from plastic cups as they sat around tables on the sidewalk.

He gave me a nod as I walked up. "Travers. Haven't seen you in years. How's your old man? You come to join the league?"

"Team sports still aren't my thing."

"Don't know what you're missing, man."

"Cheap beer and a participation trophy?"

"League champions trophy this season. Comes with a T-shirt." He plucked at the shirt he wore, displaying the screen-printed logo.

"I stand corrected."

Dave grinned and turned to one of his buddies at the table. "This here is Greyson Travers. Top of his class at the Academy."

"You still with the department?" the friend asked.

I shook my head. "Never was."

"Travers paid his own way. The city offered to pick him up but he turned them down," Dave explained. "Decided to go the private route."

"Police work wasn't for me," I said.

The friend shrugged. "Some guys don't have it."

"Want a beer?" Dave asked.

"I'll get this round. Let me pick your brain about a case."

"Deal," he said. Dave gestured to the other guys around the table. "You guys need one?"

Thanks to the Wednesday night special on domestics, a round for six guys and myself only cost me twenty bucks. I overtipped the bartender and she brought them out to us.

I showed Dave a picture of Foster and Isla Phillips and he filled me in on the details of the case he could share. He hadn't been the only one working it but was convinced it was by the book.

"Trust me, I'd have kept the case open if there was anything to go on. Didn't mind that Mrs. Phillips coming by one bit. But handwriting analysis had a clean match. We had plenty of samples. Note said plain as day that he was doing himself in. We dusted everything. House, car. Blood spatter analysis, fibers, bank records, phone records. The works. The widow swore it was foul play but they all want it to be something it's not. Collect your fee and move on to the next one."

"Gunpowder residue?"

"Now that I recall, that was one thing we came short on. Not much on his hands. But it was on scene. Trust me, Grey, we did the diligence."

"The victim had a record. Any chance his death was connected to his past?"

"Wouldn't have thought so. Unless he was hiding worse than we know about. Had a dishonorable discharge from the Army. Maybe something there, but we don't see many guys get a guilty conscience and go offing themselves over small time shit he was into. Maybe he wanted away from her. Lots of people get depressed. It happens. The guy said as much in the note."

"They checked the note for prints, I assume."

"Sure. Just his. Right there on the desk for all to see. Like I said. Open and shut. Suicide."

"What was his explanation? In the note."

Dave furrowed his brow. "Don't recall it saying much. Just something about . . . it was his time to go."

I finished my beer.

That time for me too.

I looked around for my cat when I got home to Friday afternoon. He wasn't in his usual spot on the patio wall but must have been recently. The mail carrier had left the mail on the bottom step. Hawk had once again discouraged her from making it all the way to the mailbox.

I climbed the concrete steps to my garage apartment and pressed my thumb to the fingerprint sensor on the door. I took one last look for the cat, then reached inside the door for the tin of cat treats. I shook it. Hawk shot out of the bushes in the neighbor's yard.

"Keeping the world safe from vermin?"

Hawk meowed.

I set a handful of treats on the concrete wall that rimmed my small front porch. He leapt up and immediately set to devouring them, purring like a well-tuned motor.

I went inside.

I walked to the bedroom and collapsed onto my bed. Kicked off my shoes.

My chronometer was next. I placed it on the charging pad hidden in the surface of the nightstand. Sunglasses too. I folded my hands across my chest and closed my eyes but my mind wouldn't settle. After a minute of futility, my eyes opened again.

"Waldo, I have some new video recordings on my phone. The Phillips residence. Compile them for me and add in the feed from my sunglasses cam too. A couple of dudes in a Mercedes G-Class rubbed me the wrong way. Get whatever background you can on the guys in the video, will you?"

His voice came from the room's built-in sound system. "Would you like me to do any more of your job for you while you enjoy your nap?"

"Yes. I need a new assistant. Find your replacement for me."

"I've done a comprehensive search of applicants in neighboring centuries. There is an abacus from 1880 willing to give you a chance. Shall I send for it?"

"Wake me when it shows up."

I gave the siesta a solid effort, but was awake within an hour.

Something about what Dave had said didn't sit right. I just didn't know why. I'd hoped the hour of sleep might sort whatever my conscious mind had missed, but no such luck. I was back to doing legwork.

I climbed off the bed and went to the kitchen, mixed myself a drink.

Old Fashioned in hand I walked back to my bedroom and opened the closet.

My plans for the night didn't call for anything specialized, so I donned a pair of dark jeans, a light-blue button down, a navy blazer, plus faux leather wing-tip oxfords and a belt to match. I looked damned good.

Everything I was wearing had already been treated for time traveling, imbued with temporally unusual particles known as gravitites. Besides natural charisma, the particles in my body were what set me apart from linear men. A chronometer on an average person's wrist would be nothing more than a flashy decoration.

Stuff with gravitites can time travel, stuff without them can't.

It's a simple rule that new travelers are wont to forget, causing them to arrive at their destinations stark naked, leaving piles of belongings behind when they vanish. Never a classy look. I fitted my recharged chronometer back to my wrist, slipped on my shades, finished my drink, and locked up the apartment.

Waldo had summoned me a ride and it was already pulling up to the curb.

It was time to revisit the Phillips' house.

4

Isla Phillips opened the front door wearing a dress that could start a riot—a billowy maxi-length number the color of a Georgia peach. The laces holding the plunging V-neck together weren't good at their job. I glued my eyes to her angelic face.

"You came." Her flushed cheeks were framed by waves of black hair.

"The invitation was irresistible."

She held up a glass that was mostly ice. "You missed the first round. You'd better catch up."

"Had one before I left. But hit me again."

She led me into the kitchen where indie rock streamed from the sound system.

Can lights illuminated a countertop tiled in a Moroccan motif. Stainless basin sink and a pot-filler spigot. Modern appliances with touchscreen interfaces.

"Cocktail or beer?"

"Whatever's coldest and wettest."

Isla opened the fridge and pulled out a bottle of Cigar City Lager. "Foster liked these."

"Have to appreciate a guy who drinks local."

My host selected a can of White Claw for herself but went to the effort of pouring it over her glass of ice.

She caught me staring. "You like the dress?"

"Not going to thank it for obscuring an otherwise excellent view."

Isla turned. "You talk to all the grieving widows you meet this way?"

"If it's welcomed. You want me to pretend it's not?"

She studied me in silence for a long moment, then turned on her heel and led me through the sliding doors to the back lanai, the dress swishing about her ankles.

There was a pool with lights that changed colors at the bottom, built-in planters around the deck. Cantina lights were strung above an outdoor bar—an inviting space. Beyond the screen enclosure was a well-kept lawn. I had a hard time imagining Isla behind a push mower but someone was taking good care of it all.

"Great place. How long have you lived here?"

She took a seat at the outdoor bar, gliding onto the stool and resting her drink on the bar top. I mounted a stool beside her. "A few years. It's a work in progress."

"LinkedIn had Foster's job title listed as 'freelance security.' Does that pay better than I've been led to believe?"

Isla ran a forefinger along her perfectly formed lips and over her chin in a way that wasn't distracting at all. "Foster worked a lot of jobs. Personal security was one. Is looking into our finances part of your investigation?"

"I'm rude and I like to pry."

Isla laughed. "I don't believe you. You don't seem the type of man who talks for no reason. I admire that."

My heart turned a somersault.

"I purchased the house a few years before Foster and I were married. When I started work at the casino."

"What kind of work do you do for them?"

"Admin really. Sort of a concierge position. I fit certain players to the games they'd most enjoy. My clients mostly prefer high stakes poker."

I made a mental note to investigate that further.

"Do you know anyone who wanted to harm Foster? Or any vices that might have got him into trouble? Drugs?"

"No. He never did any. Might have smoked once or twice with friends but it wasn't his thing. He drank but never lost his head. He was used to not drinking around others who were."

"Like you?"

She paused the drink on the way to her lips. "Mostly. I'm not one to waste a night off. But he'd probably agree with me now."

"Life is short. Did he behave like he wanted a future?"

"God yes. He was always looking up dream vacation spots. Tropical beaches mostly. Even the morning of the day he died. I found a listing on his phone. We didn't have a proper honeymoon when we were married, but he wanted to take me on one. I think he was trying to surprise me with a trip. I tried telling the police there was no way he would plan a vacation like that and then kill himself. Wouldn't you agree?"

"It would be helpful if I could see his phone. You still have it?"

"In the bedroom. They gave his things back when they closed the case."

"It seems like you're doing well financially. Why no honeymoon?"

"My job demands a lot of my time. Clients are high profile and can be high maintenance. The management prefers that I keep myself available."

"How did Foster feel about that?"

Isla shrugged one shapely shoulder. "He wished we were the ones on the other side of the table. But we were happy enough."

"Can you walk me through the location where his death happened? Unless it's too emotional for you."

"No. Thank you. I'm fine." She knit her fingers around her cocktail glass. "I want you to have everything you need."

She glided off the stool and led the way back inside. The music seemed louder.

We turned left past the kitchen and she took me down a brief hallway that split to meet several doors. The master bedroom door was ajar and revealed an elegantly outfitted king bed neatly made with a mountain of decorative pillows. The office door was to my left and it was there that she guided me.

The desk was reclaimed wood. Three drawers with a slim silver monitor on top. A small lamp. Cords were all tightly bundled down the back. There was an armchair, a bookcase, an oval throw rug beneath the ottoman. Office chair was missing. Exercise ball sat in one corner.

"Would you say your husband was a tidy man?"

"Absolutely. Always kept his office like this. Nothing out of place."

"What about the day he died?"

Isla's cheeks grew taut as she clenched her jaw. She pointed to an area just left of the desk. "He was in his office chair. There. I threw it out because I couldn't . . . his blood—"

"It's okay. You don't have to talk about it. If you could find the phone, I'd like to look at that."

Isla wiped under one eye to catch a tear, smearing her eyeliner. "It was just like this. Only that chair—I'll get the phone." She spun out of the room and her dress wafted after her as she vanished.

Whoever had cleaned up had done a good job. The fresh paint was barely discernible on the wall where they'd patched a bullet hole.

Isla returned with the phone and disabled the security timer before passing it over. "Will you have to look through the photos? I haven't had a chance to check if there's anything . . . private on there."

"You can take me through any relevant photos yourself, make sure we bypass anything of a delicate nature."

"Yes. Thank you. If you can excuse me, I need to . . ." She gestured to her smeared eyeliner.

"Please do. I'll only be a few minutes." As she vanished into the master bedroom, I closed the office door behind her.

I thumbed through the unlocked phone of Foster Phillips, skimming the various apps he had installed. Nothing unusual. The open browser windows weren't illuminating either. The news app. A few social media sites. A vacation rentals site. He had several places bookmarked. They did look tropical. Maybe Mexico. I checked his calendar. It was mostly blank after the day of his death. The only upcoming event noted was this coming Sunday. WORK TRIP. No time or destination was specified.

Not going to be making that.

That was all the cards he had showing. If this was a poker hand, I'd fold.

I flipped to the photos and checked for images of Foster's house, using only the search bar and typing first "office" then "desk." It was only when I tried "chair" that I finally had a hit that showed the home office I was in now. The rolling office chair had no arms and was tucked tightly against the desk. A smiling Foster Phillips grinned back at the camera from a standing position. Alive. This photo showed him with an amused smile. Dark hair, dark eyes. An intensity of focus to his gaze.

Another shot showed the office again, this time without him in it. Tidy. Like Isla said.

Okay. I would take the risk.

I double-checked the time on the phone. As much as I enjoyed Isla's company, it was time to work. Time to visit the scene of the crime. I studied each photo of the office I could find and selected the space that was consistently unoccupied. I set the phone on the desk, then dialed my chronometer settings and pressed my hand to the edge of the bookshelf. It was time to see how Foster Phillips died.

I pushed the pin.

5

The man in the chair was certainly dead.

I hated this part of the job.

I'd arrived back on the date of Foster's suicide, the minute after I heard the gunshot in the Phillips' house. Outside, two men lurked in a blacked-out SUV and an earlier version of me was standing in the alley on the next block recording the time. Soon he'd jump back to the future to make his way to becoming present me. Twisty time travel.

Death doesn't bother me but this scene did. Foster Phillips was staring blankly toward the wall beyond his desk with a piece of his head missing. Despite any troubles he'd had with the law, he was a young man with a beautiful wife and a promising future.

There was less blood than I expected. Not like TV.

I didn't move. Just observed. I only had a few minutes till Isla showed up.

I slipped my sunglasses on and hit record as I studied the scene.

Learn fast.

I scanned the room. Foster's body, still warm. The desk had a laptop open. A browser window showed the same vacation listing he'd had on his phone. A loose pen cap rested on the desk with no sign of the pen. A half-empty glass of water sat on a coaster. A drop of blood had spattered onto the outside of the glass. Otherwise the desk was uncluttered. I didn't touch a thing.

This was the most dangerous part of what I did.

Jumping through time in an unfamiliar location is a good way to wind up fused with a piece of furniture. That's bad enough. But the act of inserting myself into a known past is every bit as dangerous. People think time is a straight line—the actions of a concrete history creating the fleeting present ahead of an amorphous and undefined future. They're wrong on all counts.

Time isn't a straight line, it's a fractal, capable of being broken or altered at any point. But while an infinity of variations could exist, it's a finite number that actually does. The reality of a "present" is an illusion, though as Einstein suggested, a very persistent one.

A good time traveler always walks the past like a crime scene, careful of his footsteps.

Unless the police report mentioned a private detective with classic movie star good looks being present at the time of their arrival, I had to be gone when they got here. Anything else would mean a paradox, or possibly a change to time. Not what I was there to do.

Observe. Take notes. Don't disturb anything.

At least that was the plan until the man in the balaclava stepped through the doorway.

Thankfully I'm bad at shrieking or I might have tried it.

I'd been focused on keeping my cool with the scene before but now I mimicked an ice sculpture. Froze in place.

Who was this guy?

He didn't notice me at first, intent as he was on the body in the chair.

He stooped to have a look at the weapon on the floor beneath

Foster's limp arm. Looked like a Glock 23 from where I stood. Then the man looked up.

Perhaps it was a function of the ski mask over his face but when his eyes went wide, he looked cartoonish.

His hand still hovered near the planted gun.

My fingers flew to my chronometer, dialing my destination as fast as I could. I expected him to go for the gun again. I had time. But he raised his other hand instead. Something invisible struck me in the chest. My stomach spasmed, my legs turned to jelly, and I lost muscle control. I hit the floor hard, gasping for breath. It wasn't a stun gun. Something worse. My mind flickered, sight coming and going as my consciousness fought to stay.

He stepped closer. Not a big guy, but a giant from my perspective. He loomed over me and aimed his gloved palm at me again. Something at its center glowed. "Whoever you are, you're a dead man."

"Not yet," I muttered. My hands were beneath me on the floor. My fingers found the pin on my chronometer and I pressed it.

The image of the man standing over me vanished as I catapulted myself forward through time. When I arrived, my body was still reeling from whatever I'd been hit with and my chronometer was scalding hot, burning my wrist. I fumbled with the latch and the chronometer clattered to the floor. I hissed through my teeth as I rubbed my wrist and stayed curled in the fetal position on the floor.

Shit. That hadn't gone well.

I checked my arm. A burn in the shape of forked lightning had spread from my wrist halfway to my elbow.

I unclamped my jaw and rolled onto my side with a groan. I located the chronometer and shoved it into my jacket pocket. I was only just feeling like I could try moving again when the door opened and Isla Phillips appeared in the doorway.

"Jesus, are you okay?"

"Not Jesus," I muttered as I climbed to my feet. "But people confuse us all the time. Same great abs."

She must not have found me funny. Maybe her ears were ringing too.

"What happened?"

"Nothing. Dizzy spell."

"What can I get you?" Isla asked. "You look like you should sit down."

She guided me out of the office and back to the living room. "Are you on something? You need a doctor?"

"No. I'm fine. One too many is all."

By the time I reached the couch I was steadier. Enough that I declined the seat. My body aches were letting up and the effects from whatever had hit me were dissipating.

"I'm staying right next to you till we're sure. What about some fresh air?" She led me back outside, this time to a wicker loveseat near the pool.

Once we were seated she leaned close and put a hand to my arm. "Are you sure you're okay? If you need something..."

"Better now. But I've discovered a few things. One is that your husband was murdered."

Her breath caught.

Isla Phillips was a strong woman. It was evident in the natural grace she exhibited. Grace doesn't thrive on its own in the modern world. It must be projected from strength. But even strong women have limits.

My words settled into her. Changed something.

"How? Why?"

"Don't know yet."

"But you're sure. Murdered."

It wasn't a question, but I nodded.

She let out the breath and her shoulders slumped. "You have proof to give the police?"

"Not yet. But I'll get it."

"If you need to keep the phone longer . . ."

She thought I'd found my proof on her husband's phone. Of course she did. What else could I have been doing in a closed office? Certainly not getting knocked down by a guy six months ago.

"That would be helpful. I'd like to hang onto it for a day if I can."

She nodded. Wrung her hands. "I'll reset the password before you leave. Will you stay a bit longer? I'm worried about you leaving in the state you're in."

"I do have a few more questions."

"Ask me anything."

"Why him?"

She met my eyes, questioning, but seemed to understand. She took a breath. "He was . . . different. Not what I was used to. He had this incredible assuredness about him. I think part of me just wanted to see what that was like."

"You weren't used to confident guys?"

Her expression darkened. "I was used to entitled assholes. Foster wasn't like that. He'd worked for everything he had."

"Any of these entitled assholes ever come around while you were married to Foster?"

"Occasionally on the job. But never outside of work. Foster would run them off. He wasn't shy about that. Didn't tolerate other guys hitting on me. He could be a bit . . . possessive."

"Violent?"

"Never with me."

"But you tolerated it."

"It's not the worst thing. A man who fights for what's his. He made me feel like I was his whole world. I felt . . . protected."

"How long did you date before you were married?"

Isla bit her lip. Held her breath. Her response came out with her exhalation. "Two weeks."

I tried to stay stoic but my raised eyebrows betrayed me.

"We were doing something spontaneous. But we really had a connection. It wasn't as crazy as it sounds."

I ruminated on that. "Somebody wanted your husband dead, Mrs. Phillips. Who do you think that was?"

Isla fidgeted with a bracelet on her wrist. "I don't know."

She knew something but I didn't push her. Not yet.

"That a charm bracelet?"

Isla looked down at the bracelet she'd been fidgeting with and stopped. "It was a gift. He used to call me his lucky charm. It's from a quote he saw at the casino the night he met me. I know it's not the style anymore but it was something he gave me that felt real."

She had a slight hitch in her voice. It sounded authentic. She turned back to me with moist eyes. "How do you know he was murdered? What's your proof?" Her face was expectant, vulnerable. She needed hard evidence and something to validate her faith in me.

"I'm playing that close to the chest for now. Still working out the details. But I'll get justice for Foster. I don't know what that looks like yet, but I promise you'll have it."

She seemed mollified by that.

Isla gathered herself and rose. We wandered back indoors.

I sipped water and oozed competence. The unflappable calm of the stalwart detective.

Isla was still attentive. Would I like another beer? Stay a little longer?

I wanted both but the nagging in my head wouldn't let me.

Despite my rampaging confidence, all I really had to show for the night was a busted chronometer, a sore body, all the signs of an impending hangover, and a dead guy's phone.

Nothing good ever happens after midnight, and getting there in the proximity of Isla Phillips wasn't going to do anything for my mental clarity.

It was time to go.

Isla walked me to the door.

"Call me tomorrow?" she said.

"I'll check in," I said. "Goodnight."

I summoned a ride on my phone.

Standing on the curb, I stared up at the few stars the trees and light pollution couldn't obscure. I wondered what the rest of the universe was up to tonight. It was only as the Uber was arriving that I noticed the shifting silhouette in the driver's seat of an eighties model Dodge truck down the street.

I climbed into the passenger seat of my rented ride and watched the side mirror.

"Back to the Burg?" the driver asked.

She was hipper than me.

"In no particular hurry," I said.

She shifted the car back into drive and pulled away. A block behind us the Dodge slunk out of its parking space. Its lights didn't come on until we were turning the corner.

Looked like my night wasn't over.

6

My Uber driver needed to invest in better air freshener. The label on the container said 'dark cherry' but smelled like someone burning Fruit Loops in a Yankee Candle store. I cracked the window and checked the side-view mirror again. The Dodge truck was two cars back on the interstate, keeping a wary distance.

I had the driver drop me off near my office downtown instead of my apartment. Central Avenue was busy. Couples held hands strolling beneath the streetlights and groups of twenty-somethings laughed their way between bars. My Uber driver had a new fare by the time I got out of the car.

I pretended to ignore the Dodge as I walked up the block. Whoever was tailing me would have a hard time finding parking downtown on a Friday night. Despite the glacial 15 mph speed limit, they were forced to pass my position on the sidewalk. I made sure there was a palm tree between us as they went by in case they were looking to shoot me, but the driver was doing a good job of pretending to be uninterested.

I stole a glance. Guy. Mid-thirties. Scruffy beard and a trucker hat. Never seen him before.

The truck was a beater. Faded blue paint and rust holes on the bed. I pulled my phone from my pocket and made a note of the license plate number. I'd see what Waldo could do with it.

The burrito place next door to my office was still open so I stood in line at the take-out window and waited for Trucker Hat to reappear. Took about five minutes but I spotted him across the street just about the time my tempeh burrito was up. What to do.

This guy clearly had an interest but wasn't especially subtle about it. Still, he was one of the only leads I had going at the moment. It wouldn't pay to lose him.

I opened the door to my office and locked it again from the inside, then jogged up the stairs two at a time. When I reached my office I stole a quick peek out the window to see if my stalker was still on the corner. He was. I noted the time and sat myself at the desk to see what I could do with my chronometer.

First things first. I ate the burrito. No good working on an empty stomach.

The tool kit was in the credenza. Once the burrito was gone, I made short work of opening the back of my chronometer and inspecting the damage. Easy to find. The capacitor for storing excess static had overloaded and separated at its seams. Whatever I'd been hit with at Isla's was meant to do more harm than I'd received. The capacitor had taken the brunt of it. Might have saved my life.

I retrieved a spare capacitor from my parts kit and used the magnifying lamp to do the requisite surgery. I had the chronometer back together in fifteen minutes.

Test trip.

I stood and put my fingertips on the rings that selected the time. Then I double-checked my pockets for anything that wouldn't make the jump. Found Foster's phone in my jacket. I stuffed it into a drawer of my desk.

"Hey Waldo, you awake?"

"You know how I love it when you ask questions you already

know the answers to." His voice droned from the speaker in the desk lamp.

"What time did I leave the office this morning?"

"Eleven forty-one AM. Eastern Standard Time."

I set my chronometer for 11:42.

"See you this morning." I touched my chronometer hand to the desk, noted the time on the wall clock, and pressed the jump pin.

The onslaught of daylight made me squint.

The office still smelled like Isla Phillips. Lovely.

My Stinger 1911 was on the desk—the exit anchor my earlier self had used to jump home. Time to clean up after myself.

I snatched up the gun and moved to the credenza. The right-hand cabinet concealed the gravitizer. Ten seconds inside was enough to imbue the gun with enough of the temporally unstable particles to make a trip in time. I took off my jacket and put on my shoulder rig while I waited. The gravitizer made a satisfying chime when the treatment was complete. I slid the pistol into the shoulder holster and donned my jacket again.

"Hey Waldo, can you research a Kentucky license plate number for me?" I read him the plate number.

"Honoring your request will again require me to circumvent local legal parameters."

"But for a good cause."

"Are you appealing to the conscience of a synthetic mind?"

"I know you have a heart of gold, Waldo. Lack of a body is a technicality."

"I'll see what I can manage."

I smiled.

Time to go meet my new friend.

I set my chronometer for shortly before my Uber driver would show up and jumped back to the nighttime. I locked up the office and trotted down the stairs.

I was across the street near the roundabout when my earlier

self arrived by Uber. He lingered in the line for a burrito while the Dodge drove by.

Tick tock tick tock. Fun with time travel.

My mystery driver made a left out of the roundabout and headed for First Avenue South. I jogged across the street to conceal myself behind the closed Thai restaurant on the southwest corner. Trucker Hat came slinking back on foot and posted up at the southeast corner, spying on the version of me in line for the burrito. I waited till my earlier self was unlocking the office door before skirting across the lot of the Thai restaurant to get a better angle on my stalker. I was peering around the rear corner of a parked car when my earlier self peeked out the blinds of the office. Once the blinds stopped moving, I was in the clear.

I had one hand on the grip of my Stinger as I jogged across the street. Trucker Hat still had his back to me, watching the office. Sweat stained the back of his Guy Harvey T-shirt. He had a buck knife in a sheath clamped to the belt holding up his Levis.

The movies always show guys jamming guns into people's backs. I wasn't that dumb. I kept my distance and raised my voice.

"See anything interesting?"

When Trucker Hat spun around, I had the Stinger leveled, waist high and aimed at his chest. He did a double take.

"I know. I was there but now I'm here. How'd I do that?" I puffed my cheeks out and mimed an explosion from my skull with my free hand.

He looked tired and rumpled. Long night of watching Isla's place?

"What do you want?" I said.

"You got the wrong idea."

"Enlighten me."

His eyes were frantic.

"Don't run," I added.

He ran.

Shit.

I wasn't above shooting people, but unarmed strangers sprinting down Central Avenue didn't make the cut. I holstered my pistol. People gave Trucker Hat odd looks as he dashed to the end of the block and raced around the corner. Headed to his truck no doubt.

I checked my phone. A notification showed Waldo's info on the license plate was there in the data cloud. Truck was registered to a Dirk P. Walls. Dirk. That's a name you don't hear often. A quick check of the time showed I still had a few minutes till my earlier self would be done fixing the chronometer in the office. I walked across the street and ordered a beer from the burrito place. When my watch hit the appropriate time, I ascended the stairs again and walked back into the office. My earlier self was gone.

"Failing at your job again?" Waldo asked.

"This one's a sprinter." I set my beer on the credenza and reset my chronometer. Before my jump, I fished around in the toolkit and came up with a slim jim that ought to work on an '80s model Ford.

Let's try this again.

I reappeared in the office prior to either of my previous visits and trudged back down the stairs. It would be a full ten minutes till I'd show up in the Uber now. Enough time to avoid my other selves. I crossed the street, followed the trail of my future quarry, and located the only open parking space on First Avenue South. Then I waited, lurking in the alley, concealed by a malodorous dumpster. Oh the glamorous life of a P.I.

Dirk Walls arrived in his battered pickup truck and parked. He walked off to stalk me.

I used the slim jim on his passenger side door and had it unlocked in seconds. I climbed into the truck and left the door ajar as I rifled through the glove box. There was a Smith and

Wesson .38 with a half box of ammo in there. It wasn't a Glock like Foster's killer had used, but maybe he had multiple guns. There were a few receipts for truck parts and several loose ketchup packets.

Man of simple tastes.

The truck was a manual. I respected that.

I closed the truck door the rest of the way and slouched in the darkened interior, taking care to flip the switch on the dome light all the way to the off position.

The minutes ticked by and I turned to keep an eye out for Dirk. First Avenue South was a one-way street four lanes wide here. The truck was parked on the left side of the road meaning Dirk would approach it from the left rear. We were a good distance from the nearest streetlight and he'd have a minimal view of the passenger seat until he was climbing in. That was my hope anyway.

He showed up at a dead sprint minutes later, huffing and puffing down the sidewalk. I slid lower in the passenger seat with my hands resting across my abdomen. Dirk had to fight with the keys to get the driver's side door unlocked. He yanked the door open and didn't seem to notice that the light failed to come on. He was all the way behind the wheel by the time he saw me sit up.

"Oh shit!" He went for his knife.

I grabbed the hair at the back of his head with my left hand and slammed his nose into the top of the steering wheel. His hat fell off.

"Jeezus!"

"Time to talk, Dirk." I plucked the buck knife from his belt and tossed it to the footwell on my side.

He put a hand to his face and felt his nose. I hadn't slammed him hard enough to break anything but his eyes were watering.

"You ought to realize you can't run from me. Let's not do this dance anymore."

"What do you want?" he mumbled through his hand.

"Shut the door. Let's go for a drive. You get to tell me all about yourself."

7

Dirk P. Walls didn't seem a bad sort. His teeth would thank him if he quit the dip and he could use a more frequent hygiene regimen, but he was a man's man who knew what he was about. His truck ran well and the white fur on the seat said that a dog was a frequent resident of his passenger seat. He couldn't be all terrible.

I plucked one of the dog hairs from the seat. "You own a wolf?"

He glanced at me and then the hair. "White shepherd."

"Start talking, Dirk. What were you doing outside the Phillips' house tonight?"

"Just watching out for her is all."

"For Isla Phillips."

"Been a friend to Foster. He'd want her checked on."

"And with a heart of gold like yours, you're the man for the job." I checked the time. It was almost one o'clock. Good thing I had a siesta. "So tell me the story, Dirk. Foster takes his life, you pop round to see how the missus is doing. How often? You been by before?"

"Time or two. Nothing to trouble yourself over."

"You must think I'm an idiot. Did you not get close enough to my office to read the sign?"

Dirk Walls sucked his teeth.

"Says 'detective,'" I added, in case he wasn't getting it.

"Shit." It came out like "she-it."

"You want me to go poking around your life, pestering everyone with questions and stirring things up? It's literally my job and I'm annoying as hell."

Dirk was staring hard at the road but his mind was on my threat.

"Or you could cut the bullshit now and tell me what you were really doing there."

I let the ensuing silence work on him. Only took about a minute till he cracked.

"Foster and I had an arrangement. Just business."

"What kind?"

"Unfinished kind."

"Seems like you finished it to me."

"What? No. Not like that. You think I killed him?" Dirk's knuckles were white on the steering wheel.

"Who said he was killed?"

"Nobody. He killed his self."

"This business you had get Foster killed? You in it too? Who else?"

Dirk clenched his jaw.

"Okay. Here's how this game goes. Foster was murdered and you just shot straight to the top of my suspect list. In order to not be at the top, someone else with a motive has to bump you. Who else knew what you were into?"

"Not saying nothing else."

"That's a double negative."

"I'm done talking."

I pressed him. "There were a couple guys in a black Mercedes SUV sitting outside Foster's house the day he died. Big ugly fat one and a slick skinny one with pinched eyes. White dudes. You know 'em?"

His eyes narrowed. "No."

I'd bet he did.

"You're making me resort to poking around. Gonna be a lot of poking. Bound to run into whoever it is knows you're involved. Maybe I'll have to tell them you're involved. Either way it'll be awkward."

"Stay out of it then."

"Awkward for other people. Not me. You mostly."

"What are you gonna say to 'em?"

"I'll say Mr. Dirk P. Walls is holding out on them. Knows things he won't share."

"You're full of shit."

"How so?"

"Because Foster wasn't murdered. Did himself in."

"Sure about that?"

"Told me he was going to."

"He told you he was going to kill himself?"

"Not outright. But something like it. Said, 'You know there's a beach for the dead? That's the place I'm going.'"

"Beach for the dead."

"That's what he said. And sure enough, he did it."

"When was this?"

"Day he died."

We were up Fourth Street by now. Dirk's eyes flicked to the Burger King sign on Thirty-Eighth Avenue. Open late. Sitting outside Isla's all night must have been hungry work.

"Pull in." I gestured to the turn lane. He didn't hesitate. I reached for my wallet and extracted a few bills. I added an extra twenty and let him see it.

He eased into the line of cars waiting at the drive-thru.

"Dinner's on me if you give me a good reason you aren't Foster's killer."

"We served together. Afghanistan. In the shit."

I swore internally and gave him the cash.

Dirk chewed his lip. Ruminating on something. But he spoke again. "Foster said he had a job coming up. Something to do with the casino his old lady works at. Said he might be out of town for a bit. He wanted me to look in on her. Make sure nobody came around messing with her. You seen her. Never been a day in her life she was single when she didn't want to be."

"So you took it upon yourself to be the relationship police? What, she's supposed to consult you before she's allowed around other men?"

"Foster was my friend. Just doing what he wanted done."

"Foster's dead. What's he care now?"

"You ever knew what it was to follow orders, maybe you'd understand. There's a code. A man does what he has to for his boys. He made it sound like she might be in some kind of trouble with him gone. I told him I had his back. So him dead or not, that's what I'll do."

"I don't believe you, Dirk. I'm going to ask around about you."

"You ain't gonna find nothin'." He spit out the window.

"There you go with your double negatives again. I'll leave you now."

"Don't be telling nobody about me, you understand? I'm just doing what he wanted."

I popped the door open and climbed out. "Your secrets aren't unsafe with me." I slammed the door.

Dirk gave me a scowl. I got the impression he would have liked to roar off in a cloud of exhaust smoke, but his position in the drive-thru line precluded such a manly exit.

I revised my opinion of Dirk. Dog or no dog, he was an asshole.

8

I crossed Fourth Street via the crosswalk, then strolled south into Old Northeast. It was a fair hike to my place, but once I was off the main road and under cover of the old oaks, the walk was less of an inconvenience. I could use it. Clear my head.

My encounter with Dirk had given me another angle to this puzzle but now it was all corners and no edges. My mind kept showing me scenes from my night. Mostly Isla's lips and the gaping hole in Foster's head. Needed a good night's sleep and a fresh start.

Hawk was waiting for me at the top of my steps, his golden eyes reflecting moonlight and making him look like the predatory killer he was. I scratched under his chin till his purring got loud, then filled his food dish. It occurred to me as I navigated the hallway to my bedroom that I'd left a nearly full beer at my office. It was still cold when I left too. I was too tired to go back for it now but I did make a note on my phone. A future me wouldn't let it go to waste.

I undressed and crashed into the pillows face-first.

When my alarm went off at 7 a.m. I was still tired. I noticed the door to the guest room was locked. Not a bad idea.

I jumped back in time two hours, careful not to wake myself on arrival, went into the guest room and locked the door. I got another two hours of sleep before the alarm went off at seven again. This time I felt I could handle it.

Coffee first. Then coffee.

Breakfast was fresh fruit over oatmeal, juice, two glasses of water, and Advil. The Old Fashioned and the beers had been a great idea at the time but today would require reparations. Workout shorts and a T-shirt got me out the door. Hawk was missing again. Off regulating the local feline population no doubt. Had to keep the neighborhood hierarchy in order.

I refilled his water bowl and trotted down to the garage.

There was a sexy beast of a machine in the driveway.

The Boss.

Dad must have jumped it here sometime overnight. Never heard it arrive.

I hadn't owned a car in a decade. Wasn't anywhere I wanted to go that I couldn't get to by bicycle, rideshare, or time travel, but I had to admit the Boss had style. Dark as death and just as mean, the car's curves were an assault on decency. It had the body of a '68 Mustang fastback but had been taken to the future for upgrades. An electric auto-drive system was rigged beneath an upgraded factory engine. More importantly, it could time travel. The intake for the supercharger yawned wide like a ravenous predator. It was a vehicle that would devour its enemies and crush their bones beneath its tires. Chrome door handles and window trim were the only accents keeping it from being mistaken for a black hole.

Not a car you parked outside if you wanted the neighbors to like you.

I opened the garage to see if I could make room.

My weight bench was centered in the right-hand bay. Toolboxes and more anchor cabinets filled the left. Relocating the weight stand was a workout in itself but once I got the bench moved, I loaded the bar with two forty-five pound plates each side and pressed out a set. Not bad for a warmup. I stretched and loaded up another pair of thirty-fives, then climbed into the interior of the car to link it with the house.

It took over an hour to upload Waldo to the onboard CPU of the Boss, but it was worth it. Bouncing around time, access to the cloud could be spotty. I finished my workout while I waited.

By late morning I was freshly showered and changed, wearing my cozy stakeout clothes: a black hoodie, worn-in jeans, a T-shirt, and Chuck Taylors. I wore a ball cap and shades as well, completing the look. It was one of my ABC's of investigations. Always be comfortable.

Plus, it was Saturday.

Then, it was mid-October. Foster's death day.

Time to fit another piece in this puzzle.

I parked the Boss in Hyde Park, a block away from the Mercedes G-Class SUV and Foster Phillips' house. There were already too many of me in the vicinity today. One of me staking out the alley on foot, one showing up inside the house and getting zapped by a dude I assumed was Foster's killer, and now me, lurking in the pitch-black void of the Boss's interior.

But the events inside the house weren't what I was after this time.

Waldo commandeered the stereo, and the sounds of Kavinsky soon emanated from the speakers. He'd been on a synth wave kick lately. Better than the strange phase when he'd been into twenty-second-century emo jazz. I didn't criticize. I'd learned that A.I. developed their interests how they wanted. It was best to let them.

I watched the clock. Shortly after Foster Phillips met his maker, the black SUV rolled by. I paired my phone with the camera I'd attached to the Mercedes' side-view mirror on my first visit.

Bingo. Now I had eyes.

The Boss had a display screen on the dash so I routed the video feed to that, then pulled out of my parking space. The Mercedes had turned a corner, but thanks to my hitchhiking camera, I had a clear view of their route.

Work smarter, not harder. Dirk P. Walls should take some pointers.

The Mercedes took the Selmon Expressway to Twenty-Second Street, then the access road that wound north to the Ybor City Historic District.

Historic Ybor was once home to Tampa Bay's thriving cigar business but was now populated by breweries, nightclubs, and Scientologists. The old buildings were still there, however, and I had an inkling the Mercedes didn't belong to the L. Ron Hubbard crowd. I bumped over trolley tracks embedded in the brick-paved streets as I tailed the black SUV. The Boss got a few looks from pedestrians and I could almost see the questions in their minds. Was it a new-looking old car or an old-looking new car? I passed before they could trouble themselves further.

The Mercedes slowed in front of an all-brick factory and turned down an alley. They stopped in front of a rolling industrial door and idled. I cruised past the alley at a casual clip but pulled over once I was out of sight, not wanting to lose connection with the camera. There was no discernible activity from the SUV, but they must have messaged someone inside because the loading door opened and revealed the warehouse interior.

Men with rifles waited inside. What was this about?

I leaned close to the car's display screen to get a better look and fiddled with the camera's controls via my phone. It didn't have much range of motion, but it did zoom, so I employed that to get shots of the guards. No one I recognized. I did recognize the contraption in the center of the warehouse.

It was a shipping container of the sort carried by a train, truck, or cargo ship. The doors hung open and revealed a vacant interior. Nearly vacant anyway. I zoomed in farther to get a look at the technology rigged to the interior walls. A less observant person could be forgiven for thinking it was just a mass of electrical cables bundled to form an arch. An electronic control pad mounted to one side of the container had big knobby buttons that glowed faintly. A guard typed something into it manually. Old school.

Guards moved out of the way and the Mercedes rolled forward. Transmitters rigged to the cable bundles lit up and emitted something that made the air go wavy. In a matter of seconds the space inside the shipping container was pulsing with multicolored light. It was bright enough to obscure much of the camera's view. The SUV forged ahead into the glow and the camera went completely blind. But then, just for a fraction of an instant, there was a view of a rainy twilight sky out the other end of the container.

The camera feed went dead.

I whistled.

Time gate. Not the transportation choice of your everyday gun thugs.

"Waldo, were you watching that?"

"No. I was viewing reruns of *Knight Rider* to see if I could gain a few tips."

"Funny. You happen to catch what they typed into that keypad?"

"It was an alpha-numeric key code, part of which indicated a date and time."

"Anywhere fun?"

"One of your least favorite decades. They traveled to nineteen eighty-four."

"Damn."

Time travel law enforcement had a pretty solid grip on the twenty-second century. The twenty-first century was also managed, albeit questionably. But they listed the millennium as the border of their jurisdiction. Like all borders, there was a side criminals preferred to operate on. If you equated time travel criminal activity to the North American drug trade, the year 2000 was the US/Mexico border and the 1980s and 90s were Juarez and Tijuana.

1984.

"You will never find a more wretched hive of scum and villainy," I muttered.

"Shall I begin selecting jump coordinates?"

I shifted back into gear. "Not yet. I have a stop to make."

9

Looking the part in a decade other than your own doesn't always have to be a production. Time travelers often overdo it on dressing up for trips, and the 1980s are a fashion rabbit hole. I prefer to select a single item to suit the era and leave the rest alone. That's why the pitstop to my place here in 2019 only involved ditching my hoodie and pulling a jean jacket from the closet. I had to have something to hide my gun.

My Stinger 1911 was now resting comfortably in the shoulder rig beneath the jean jacket. Some decades require more fashion, some more firepower. The '80s required both.

As I was preparing to leave the apartment again, a text showed up on my phone.

<<< Come for dinner tonight? I'd like an update.

It was Isla Phillips. I texted back.

>>> What time?

<<< Eight. Bring wine.

>>> I'll be there.

I waited for a response slightly longer than necessary, then shoved the phone into my pocket.

. . .

The jump back in time wasn't bad. I showed up in a private parking garage I knew was secure.

A thunderstorm had come through. Street signs and tree limbs were still dripping. I cruised the streets of 1984 St. Pete with a wary unease.

The city had two reputations in the '80s. One was God's waiting room, a sleepy borough of retirees and ex-somebodies living out their golden years in peace and quiet. That rep was only the façade. Some of those old timers were ex-gangsters. Some were current gangsters. Drug planes did scud runs across the Gulf of Mexico on the regular, evading radar and dropping cocaine in Tierra Verde, a peninsula destined to become the home of the rich and powerful.

St. Pete had a direct line to New York, and 1984 was a similar gateway to the next millennium for all manner of ill-gotten gains. So I kept an eye out.

Waldo managed to snag a destination date and time when the Mercedes G-Class SUV rolled through the time gate, but he didn't get me a location. That was problematic. Still, there are only so many places in this city that you can park a shipping container concealing an illegal temporal portal.

And I had time on my side.

It was 8:33 p.m. outside the train yard. I waited forty minutes and didn't see a thing. Then it was 8:33 p.m. on the Tierra Verde causeway. I gave that almost an hour before jumping back again. At 8:37 I was parked on Eighth Ave Southeast watching the south side of the Albert Whitted Airport and a barge in the Port of St. Petersburg. Two birds, one stakeout. I got lucky.

The Mercedes SUV pulled out of the port gates, cruised past me and headed up First Street. My ride-along camera was low on juice but I was able to link with it. The view from the side-view mirror soon showed rain-slicked streets and pink neon. They were headed for the dangerous part of town.

In the next thirty years, Downtown St. Pete would be

gentrified. Movie theaters and restaurants, high-end shopping and money. But not yet. In '84 you didn't come downtown unless you wanted drugs or trouble. The SUV was out of place here so I wasn't surprised when they pulled into a U-Haul storage facility and a few minutes later a '78 Buick Skylark rolled out. Squinty and Neck Folds, my acquaintances from outside the Phillips' house, were now clearly visible through the untinted windows.

Switching cars had lost my extra eyes, so I tailed the Skylark the old-fashioned way: a few cars back and playing it casual. They cruised past rows of dive bars till arriving at a place called Annihilation. The motif was apocalyptic and patrons outside could have been extras on a *Mad Max* film. Young punks in studded leather jackets and sporting colorful Mohawks drifted in and out of a cloud of cigarette smoke. In the parking lot, a trash can was on fire.

Squinty and Neck Folds climbed out of the Skylark and were met with dirty looks from the punk set, but they entered a side door without hassle. I parked the Boss in a back alley in front of a sign that said ABSOLUTELY NO PARKING EVER! then instructed Waldo to jump the car thirty minutes into the future. It vanished.

Let the meter-maid try to ticket that.

I strolled up to the nightclub and was met with hostile glares. There was a bouncer at the door but he didn't bother to ID me. Stepping inside was like huffing an exhaust pipe. Most of the twentieth century smelled like an ashtray but here I could barely see the walls. The lighting was all neon and black lights and it seemed the owners had saved on decorating by simply hitting everything with a sledgehammer. Any surface that wasn't rubble was covered in band stickers and graffiti.

I pulled my sunglasses from my pocket and activated them before slipping them on. I looked like a D-bag walking around a bar wearing sunglasses in the dark, but they came with twenty-second-century night vision and lit up the haze for me.

It still took ten minutes to locate Squinty. Neck Folds must have gone to the head.

Whatever business they had was brief. I was there in time to watch the bartender slip Squinty a metal shot glass and a business card. He looked like he was waiting for a tip but Squinty ignored him. Bartender curled his lip and walked away.

Squinty studied the card, then drank the shot while he waited on Neck Folds. He then pocketed the card and the shot glass.

Odd.

Kleptomaniac?

When Neck Folds got back from the John, I'd started recording via my sunglasses. He repeated the process Squinty had used. Bartender gave him a card and a shot. This time I noticed he'd pulled the metal shot glass from a different shelf than he was using for his other patrons. Neck Folds likewise drank the shot and kept the shot glass, tucking it into the inside pocket of his jacket.

A puzzle. I was intrigued.

Squinty and Neck Folds headed to the back of the bar and disappeared into a hallway. I followed. I took it slow and peeked around the corner. The hallway had private booths blocked off by curtains. All the curtains were closed. Whichever one Squinty and Neck Folds had gone into, they'd done it fast enough to dodge me.

I cruised the corridor, listening to any sound that made it over the music. I pushed aside a few curtains and discovered two couples in states of undress and was cursed out by several more. No gun thugs. It was only at the end of the row that I found something promising. When I pulled aside the curtain, it showed a booth without upholstery. A chain was strung across the access and a sign on the table read CLOSED FOR REPAIR. The table was indeed damaged, a third of it missing, but it hardly seemed notable considering the state of the other decor.

But Squinty and Neck Folds were nowhere to be seen.

Their two shot glasses were upended on the table.

Fascinating. This was a game I wanted to play.

I walked back to the bar and leaned on it. The bartender wandered over.

I stared at him, pushed my sunglasses up to my forehead so he could see my eyes. I was about to speak when he gave me a nod.

He turned and reached for a shot glass. He poured me some Mariachi Añejo and slid it and a business card across the bar. He then pulled a rocks glass from a stack, added a large ice cube and stuck a lime on the edge. He set that in front of me and wandered off to serve other customers.

Curiouser and curiouser.

I picked up the business card. It looked unexceptional. The name read THE LAST NIGHTCLUB and listed a phone number. On the back was a stamped jumble of letters. Furrowing my brow caused my sunglasses to slide down my forehead and land on my nose again. I poured the tequila into the rocks glass and sipped it while I studied the back of the card.

It wasn't a word jumble. My guess was a substitution cipher. Where was the key?

I turned over the metal shot glass and peered at it over the rim of my sunglasses. When I angled it toward one of the black lights, it revealed an addition sign, the number four, and the words BOTTOMS UP.

Aha.

I worked out the business card cipher on a napkin, simply jumping four positions in the alphabet for every letter. Then I pressed my sunglasses back into place against the bridge of my nose.

The result was TEN THIRTY FIVE PM EST. It didn't list a location or date. I left a ten-dollar bill on the bar and walked to the back corridor again. I dodged a staggering drunk and made my way to the empty booth. I slid the curtain closed and studied the position of the two shot glasses Squinty and Neck Folds had left behind. I replaced theirs with mine.

Bottom side up.

I set my chronometer for ten thirty-five eastern, yesterday. Then I jumped.

Then I regretted it.

10

I wasn't in Florida anymore. That's the exciting part about time travel. Seeing new sights.

I'd landed on a stool. Same height and distance relative to my shot glass but the bar was long and polished.

This wasn't a post-apocalyptic dive in the Grand Central District. Judging from the skyline view out the windows past the bar, I was in New York City. Top floor of somewhere hip and expensive.

The metal shot glass was still at my fingertips. My anchor in time. Only it was in a new location so I was too.

Fun with time travel.

I surveyed the room and noted roughly thirty people. I took off my sunglasses. No one seemed surprised by my abrupt arrival. The bartender was here. Same one from the dive in St. Pete. His wasn't a look of recognition. But how could it be? This was yesterday and he was meeting me for the first time.

He walked over and eyed me. "Welcome to the Last Night Club. What's your drink order?"

"Hook me up with a sipping tequila," I said. He poured me a

double-shot of Mariachi over an ice cube and garnished it with a lime, same way as he'd do tomorrow. He slid it to me.

"Thanks." I passed him another ten. Expenses were starting to add up.

I swiveled on my bar stool and took in the scene.

Tables. A few booths. Servers in black aprons cruised the room handing out cocktails.

There. Back wall. Watching me. The source of my unease.

He was handsome. Actual movie star handsome. His face was a pristine black with perfectly shaped eyebrows and a strong, clean shaven jaw. He completed his debonair look with a ten-thousand-dollar suit, manicured nails, and a stare that didn't waver. The women at his table were gorgeous. Could have been models. But I didn't take my eyes off the man in the suit.

From the outside, there was no visible sign that he was the center of the gravity of this room. Patrons bantered and meandered about. Conversations hadn't so much as paused at my arrival. But his eyes had found me instantly. I slid off the bar stool and walked toward him. One doesn't veer away from a singularity.

Partway to the table I was blocked by a value-sized Incredible Hulk. All the muscles at half the height.

"It's all right, Leo. Let him through. I don't think Mr. Travers is here to harm me."

Mini Hulk obeyed.

This guy knew my name. Not shy about letting me know it.

He was wearing a signet ring on his left hand emblazoned with the symbol of a pegasus.

"What's your business here, Mr. Travers?"

"You know my name but I don't know yours."

"And here I thought you were a detective." He cocked an eyebrow.

"When manners fail."

"Far be it from me to deprive you of your curiosity."

A test.

I scanned the table, his clothing, the mirror behind him, then brought my attention back to his face. The women to either side of him eyed me cautiously.

"You're Roman Amadeus."

He broke a smile, displaying impossibly white teeth. "So you are a detective. Care to divulge what gave me away?"

"There is an edge of a chronometer peeking out of the cuff of your sleeve. A limited edition Manembo chronometer that wasn't sold to you. By your ring, you attended the Academy of Temporal Sciences and were a member of the Immortal Realm fraternity so we've narrowed you down from being just a rich time traveler to being a rich, well-educated, well-connected, time traveler. But since Manembo would never have sold you that chronometer, you are either a thief or you associate with them. Add that we're in Lower Manhattan, and you're the owner of this club, the family crest over the bar makes you an Amadeus. Most of the senior members of the family are stuck in Rookwood prison or an alternate timeline for the foreseeable eternity and the only remaining cousins with brains enough to graduate the academy were all women. Except one. Roman Amadeus."

Roman nodded. "I'd like to think that a few of my male family members could have persisted through the Academy, but you're probably right. Their talents lie in other areas. How do you know the personal politics of Abraham Manembo?"

"Family friend."

"Ah. I should have guessed. Ladies, why don't you give us the table so Mr. Travers can sit down." The women beside him scooted out of the booth as fast as their miniskirts and the norms of modesty would allow.

I eased into the booth and mini Hulk squeezed himself into the other side. He caught Roman staring at him.

"What?"

"I assure you I'm quite safe, Leo. Why don't you see if Mr. Travers could use another drink."

"Oh. All right." He got back up. "You want a steak? Steak's good here."

"I'm fine, thanks."

"You should try the rib eye. Maybe the fillet."

"Leo, Mr. Travers was raised at the far end of the next century. He'd probably only accept plant-based options."

"Plant what now?" Leo scrunched his face then looked at me. "Oh like vegetarianism? Shit. Wouldn't catch me going there then. Too hard. How you live like that?"

"The key to most "isms" is not being a dick about it," I said. "The rest is practice."

Leo still didn't move. "Where you get your protein?"

I sighed. "Where do you get your flavonoids?"

His brow wrinkled. "Huh?"

"Leo." Amadeus' voice had an edge this time. "Get lost."

Leo rolled his shoulders but nodded. "Right. Sure thing, boss."

When he was gone, Amadeus sighed. "My apologies about that. Leo is a local. We're working on his social skills."

"You seem to know a lot about me. I explained my trick. What's yours?"

Amadeus shrugged. "It's my business to know these things."

"What business is that?"

"Time management."

I leaned back in my seat. "We all have that job."

"I'm better at it than most."

Roman Amadeus seemed at ease so I decided to play things straight.

"Came here tonight on the tail of two guys who used a portable time gate in late 2018." I pulled my phone from my pocket and displayed a photo taken from my sunglasses cam.

"They were lurking around a client's house. I assume they're yours."

Roman took a glance at the phone.

"You want to meet them?" He lifted a hand and gestured to the barman. The bartender put down a bottle and hurried over.

"Yes, sir?"

"Quinn, I'd like you to get a hold of Tommy Garcia and Magic Max. Send them an invite, will you? Five minutes."

"I'll make it happen."

Amadeus turned to me. "There you go. Happy to assist with whatever you need, Greyson. Do you mind if I call you Greyson?"

I had to give him credit. He was two steps ahead of me. Now if I asked why these thugs were showing up to see him, he'd say it was to meet me. A tidy causal loop.

"You have an interest in Foster Phillips."

I caught a hint of change in his expression. It passed in an instant.

He sipped his drink and set it back down. "Do you know what the most valuable commodity in the world is, Greyson? It's time. So many people in this world chase all the wrong things."

"Still runs out," I said. "No one can buy more."

"That's where I'll politely disagree. But I think it's a shame to see a man wasting his time."

Implying me, no doubt. But I didn't get a chance to reply.

Two men arrived at the bar, appearing out of thin air. There was no fanfare. No noise. One moment the stools were empty, the next they weren't.

The two men surveyed the room with an air of curiosity. Must not be regulars. They located Amadeus' table and slid off their stools. The squinty one eyed me quizzically as he walked up. Neck Folds looked even bigger out of the SUV. I'd underestimated his height.

"Gentlemen. So glad you could join us. This is Mr. Greyson

Travers, a private investigator. He has some questions for you. Greyson, meet Tommy 'The Tank' Garcia and Magic Max."

"You two have a show in Vegas?" I asked.

"That's your question?" Squinty was apparently Max. Couldn't imagine anyone labelling him Tank. And it was hard to think of his friend as anything else now that I'd seen all of him. Max had a diamond stud in his right ear I hadn't noticed before.

"What were you doing outside the Phillips' house tonight?" It was technically thirty-four years from now but he knew what I meant.

"Looking for a dog. Named Barkley." His eyes were flint.

So he did recognize me. I hadn't expected a real answer. "I'd bet you lost something more expensive than a dog."

Max flinched and glanced to Amadeus before clenching his jaw. "Don't know what you're talking about."

It was Roman's turn to narrow his eyes. With the fire behind his stare, I was surprised Magic Max didn't spontaneously combust.

Hit.

If this was Battleship, something on their side was smoking. Only time would tell if I'd struck the carrier or the PT boat.

Roman motioned with a casual wave of his wrist. Tommy and Max got the message and faded back to the bar, their looks to me all shivs and switchblades.

Roman fiddled with the pegasus ring on his finger. "You have a reputation in this community, Travers. Your family has a reputation. We have that in common. We come from significance."

I sipped my tequila. Waited.

"Significance in this world comes with respect. Your family, my family. We have our own rules. So when I tell you a thing, I know you'll think of them, you'll think of that respect."

"I can hardly stand the suspense."

Roman cocked an eyebrow. "You're smart, Greyson. And if you stay smart, you'll leave this thing alone."

"Foster Phillips is dead."

"A tragedy." Roman shrugged. "It happens."

"It was murder."

"The police ruled suicide. Suicide is . . . simpler."

"For you?"

"For everyone. Leave this to me. I absolve you of it. No longer your problem." He wiped his hands on his napkin. Dabbed at his mouth.

"And if I make it my problem?"

"I'd say that means something. About respect." He clenched the napkin in his fist. His knuckles were bloodless.

I got up. "Thanks for the drink. I'll be going."

Amadeus affixed a polite smile back to his face and signaled the bartender again. "I'll have Quinn arrange you an exit."

"No thanks. I can find my own way out."

"It's been a pleasure, Greyson. I do hope you'll drop in again." Amadeus didn't get up.

Tommy the Tank and Magic Max glared at me from the bar. Tommy was flexing.

Guy needed another hobby.

The elevator was at the back of the restaurant.

Could I have trusted Amadeus' man to find me a jump location back to tomorrow? Probably. But I wasn't going to risk it.

The ground floor lobby let out onto Stone Street in the financial district.

It was a cold night. Chilled the blood. I could see my breath.

There was history here, a dark cobblestone avenue dating back centuries stuck right in the hub of modern commerce. Modern for '84 anyway. The gutter smelled like motor oil and mothballs. I walked toward the Goldman Sachs building, pulled earbuds from my pocket, and popped one into my ear so I could communicate with Waldo.

The first earbud was barely in when Waldo spoke. "Someone is tailing you."

That's when I noticed I had a tail.

Half a block back. Trench coat. Slouchy but he couldn't hide his size. Could have been a linebacker.

Should have figured.

"Thanks, buddy."

"Would you like me to call for assistance?"

"I'm offended by the suggestion." I pocketed the earbuds again.

The good thing about Stone Street in the eighties was that it already resembled a dark alley.

I found a dead-end walkway and ducked down it. Looked like as good a place as any to get jumped. Never let it be said that Greyson Travers didn't do things right. A detective had to have some kind of standards.

When my tail came around the corner, I punched him in the throat.

11

————

P ro tip: When you are fighting in a back alley, throw out the rule book.

There's nothing like a good throat punch to get a guy's attention.

I hadn't crushed his windpipe, but the guy did make a lot of funny noises as I hit him with a flurry of jabs and a right hook that sent him to the sidewalk. He also got a kick to the gut as he tried to crawl away. That made him roll over so I could stomp on his knee.

I considered just shooting him to make my life easier. Less exertion. I pulled my Stinger from its shoulder holster and aimed it at his face. "Any last words?"

"Tee . . . See . . . Eye . . . Dee," he gasped.

"Those are some stupid last words. But it's your funeral."

He was fishing in his coat for something. The coat had fallen open, revealing a pistol in a holster at his hip, but that wasn't the side he was fumbling with. He finally got his fingers on what he was after and tossed it to my feet. The wallet fell open to reveal a badge.

I stooped and picked it up.

The badge was engraved with the letters TCID. Temporal Crimes Investigations Division.

Ah.

I could admit that his last words weren't entirely stupid.

I holstered my gun.

"We just . . .wanted . . . to talk," he wheezed.

"You're not very good at it. Your voice is all weird." I read his ID. Said his name was Theodore Baker. "Okay Teddy, where's your boss? I know you aren't the brains of this outfit."

Theodore struggled to his knees and pointed across the street. There was an unmarked van parked a half dozen cars away.

"Don't get up on my account," I said, and dropped his badge to the sidewalk again.

I crossed the street and walked up to the passenger side of the cargo van where the sliding door was. I rapped on the door with my knuckles.

It slid open and a female agent stared at me over the barrel of a .45 caliber Falcon Nighthawk. Her chestnut hair was tied back. She was wearing blue jeans, a navy T-shirt, and a bomber jacket. It was a good look. I put her in her late thirties but it was hard to tell.

Agent door-opener made an appearance too. He was an overweight, fortyish white dude, looking less cool in khakis and a beige Members Only jacket. Tough to be hip in beige. His gun was out too.

"Heard you wanted to talk."

The aviatrix lowered her Falcon by a degree. "What's your name?"

"Puddin' Tame."

She frowned. "Haven't heard that one in a while."

"Ask me again and—"

"Yeah yeah," she muttered.

"Nice surveillance van. This thing have cable?"

"Oh good. We caught a wise guy."

I scanned the interior of the van and noted a wastepaper basket full of takeout wrappers. "Looks like you've been here awhile. You find the good coffee yet?"

The agent lowered her weapon the rest of the way. "Next block over."

I said, "You're buying."

It was hard to tell if the twenty-four-hour diner was a throwback to the fifties or just hadn't been updated in thirty years. Either way, it made me want to order a milkshake.

We settled into a booth and Agent Stella York slid her business card across the table to me.

Above her name it said TIME CRIMES.

Not to be outdone, I pulled a business card from my wallet too.

She took it and snapped a photo with her phone.

Cheater.

"Travers?" Her eyebrows lifted. "You related to Benjamin Travers?"

"When I have to admit it."

She tapped the edge of the card on the table. "I thought your family stayed on the right side of the law. What are you doing coming out of a place full of known mobsters?" She pocketed my card.

"I like to stay well-rounded. How long have you been watching the Amadeus organization?"

"You say that like we ever aren't watching them. The family is into everything you can imagine. But our current interest is a money laundering scheme. We have reason to suspect Amadeus, but so far we've got nothing to pin on him. You talk to him in there?"

"You didn't get an invite?" I asked.

"TCID doesn't get asked to gangster parties."

"Sounds like it's time to quit. Make your own way in the world. Have some fun."

"That you? Lone wolf? No one to hold you accountable?"

"Many hands make more messes."

"So, private investigator. Investigating what?" She sipped her coffee and watched me over the brim.

"Dead guy. Murder. Followed a couple of Roman's gun thugs here. Just kicking the hornet's nest to see what buzzes."

"We know they're in there, but you're the only one we've seen come out. What's the trick to getting inside?"

I located the card the bartender had given me for The Last Nightclub and handed it to her. "Put a space in the word nightclub and it gets you the time. It's a space/time joke."

She studied it carefully. "Last Nightclub becomes Last Night Club. Clever. You're the first person I've spoken to that's actually been given one of these."

I wrapped my fingers around my coffee cup to warm them. "It's a pretty foolproof system. The meeting is always the night before you get the invite, so it's exclusive to time travelers. They use someone who was in attendance as a gatekeeper. If he didn't see you there the night before, you don't get access. That way only people who have been there can get there."

"What happens if the gatekeeper forgets to invite someone who already showed up?"

I shook my head. "These guys aren't amateurs. They don't strike me as the type to mess around with paradoxes. Who has you watching Amadeus?"

"ASCOTT concerns get the highest priority. My division is focused on missing time gate technology and black-market personal time travel devices."

I was familiar with the Allied Scientific Coalition of Time Travelers. The organization was the closest thing the time travel community had to a formal government. The Temporal Crimes Investigation Division was subject to their authority. They laid down the law for the use of time machines and the creation of parallel timestreams. But 1984 was well beyond their normal jurisdiction. They were going out of their way for this one.

"You think Amadeus is pulling something big?"

"Rumors on the street are that he's working for someone bigger. But we don't know all the players. Tracking these guys is like grasping at smoke. There's never any kind of paper trail and even if we catch someone in the act, there's no way to trace it to the Amadeus family."

"You tried following the money?"

"We haven't seen any change hands. These people are good."

I liked that she wasn't trying to disguise her lack of progress. She was floundering and sharing it openly. I respected that. Showed she didn't confuse setbacks with failure.

"You new to TCID? Most of the agents I've dealt with aren't so forthcoming."

Stella brushed her hair behind an ear. "Been at Time Crimes six months. Did fifteen years with the FBI before that. It was actually your grandfather who put a word in for me with the division."

"That a fact. Good to know."

"We're getting nowhere with Amadeus right now. I was planning to pull up stakes here after today if we didn't gather anything new. You learn anything we can use?"

"Roman seems to be the guy in charge. He kept things casual but made an interesting comment about time being our most valuable commodity. Thought he was speaking metaphorically, but maybe he wasn't. I'll keep digging and see what I can come up with. If you're looking for stolen time gates, I might be able to point you to one."

"You have my card," Stella said. "Maybe next time don't cripple my agents?"

"They should learn to stay on their feet."

I got up and Stella York rose with me. She had a good face. I liked her. Definitely wouldn't knock her down in an alley.

"One more thing, Travers." She brushed her hair back again. "I find you're playing both sides of this somehow, famous family or not, I'll put you away." She locked eyes with me. Held it.

I gave her a nod. "We know where we stand with each other."

"Yeah. We do."

I held the door for her.

We parted ways on the sidewalk and I noticed Agent Punching Bag glaring at me from the driver's seat of the van as I walked away. I had a feeling we weren't friends anymore.

It was going to be a pain getting back to St. Pete to pick up my car, but at least I knew where I was headed.

It was time to run down my next lead.

And I knew just where to start.

12

Waldo planned the route back to 2019 with precision and I made it without completely draining the batteries on the Boss.

It was a little after seven o'clock, Saturday evening. Still an hour till I had to be at Isla's place for dinner.

I pit-stopped at the apartment to ditch my gun and snag a bottle of wine from the rack above my fridge. Isla hadn't said what she liked. Weren't all the hip millennials drinking pinot noir these days? I didn't have one so I went with a Hedges Red Mountain cabernet. Isla deserved the good stuff.

The trip across the bridge was pleasant. I let Waldo drive. The night had cooled and we cruised through Tampa with the windows down. He shuffled some Hans Zimmer movie soundtracks, mostly from Christopher Nolan films. I took control again when we reached Hyde Park.

Isla was outside chatting with another woman when I pulled up. They both gawked at the car.

"Wow. That's sexy," Isla said as I climbed out. "New toy?"

"Spoils of war."

"Then I'd hate to be your adversary," Isla said. "What would you take of mine?"

"Whatever I can get my hands on."

Her companion was an older woman, sixties, fit and pretty. Looking uncomfortable with the conversation.

Isla introduced her as her neighbor, Jan. The woman sized me up with raised eyebrows. "Didn't know they still made men like you."

"Limited editions sometimes get a second printing."

Jan patted Isla's hand as she said goodbye. It was nice to meet me. Best get going.

Isla practically beamed at me. She had a drink in her hand. Suspected it was another White Claw over ice. Her eyes were slightly glassy, maybe not her first.

"I'm happy to see you."

I raised the wine bottle. "I come bearing gifts."

"My hero." She took me by the arm and led me toward the house. Her touch was electric. Made me feel charged and virile.

Once inside she took the bottle of wine and located a corkscrew.

There was a plate of hummus and pita chips on the kitchen island. I sampled some while she poured.

"I was worried about you after last night. Are you feeling better?"

"Nothing your pleasant company can't fix."

She handed me a glass of wine. "What shall we drink to?"

"I always drink to revenge."

"So your enemies fear you?"

"The few left alive."

"Then why don't we drink to the dead?" Her face grew serious.

"To their memory," I said, and lifted my glass. She clinked hers against it.

I took a sip. Delicious. View wasn't bad either.

Isla was wearing a billowy tunic blouse that hung off her naturally bronze shoulders. Barely visible below the shirt, she had on tight jean shorts with the sort of rips that came standard. Her legs went forever. Not that I noticed that sort of thing. She was barefoot. The bottoms of her feet could very well have been disgusting. Nothing else was.

I tried reminding myself she was a grieving widow. Didn't help.

But there was still work to do.

"The police report mentioned Foster left a note the day he died. Can I see it?"

"I told the police I didn't want it back. Couldn't stand to look at it."

"You recall what it said?"

"Hardly anything." Isla crossed one arm beneath her breasts, rested her other elbow on it, wine glass aloft. "He said goodbye. Something about it being his time. Nothing that really explained anything." She took a drink.

"Must have been difficult."

"To be honest I don't think I read it till after the paramedics came. I was too upset."

She shivered.

"I apologize for bringing up painful memories."

"No. It's what I hired you for. And you're a comfort." She uncrossed her arms, took my hand and led me to the couch.

When I sat, she sank to the cushion beside me, her leg touching mine.

I looked away to keep my mind from wandering places it shouldn't.

The house was an open floor plan, high ceilings, stylish. The room smelled of citrus. It could be the after shot of a home improvement show. Everything perfect. Until perfection shattered. I felt for her.

"You mind if we go through some of the photos on your husband's phone?" I asked.

"You really waited? I admire the self-control." She took the phone from me and screen shared with the television to make viewing easier. "What are you looking for?"

"I'd like to get a clearer picture of what Foster was like. Might help."

Isla shrugged. A gesture that she somehow made alluring. Perhaps it was the nakedness of her shoulders. She flipped through the most recent photos. Many were more screenshots of vacation rental properties somewhere warm. Farther back she encountered outings with friends and family. She narrated the events to me, naming the subjects of the shots and where they'd been taken.

I spotted a shot of Foster at a bar with friends. Place looked familiar.

"He hung out at Mastry's?"

"I thought it was a dive but he loved it. Was going for years, I think. Well before I met him. It was an oasis for him."

"How often was he there?"

"Couple nights a week?"

"He ever mention someone named Dirk Walls?"

Isla's face clouded. "The name sounds familiar. Someone from Foster's army days."

"He ever come over? Invited by Foster?"

"No. Nothing like that. Haven't heard of him in years."

I should have had more questions but her proximity was a distraction. She smelled divine.

She flipped casually through photos and spoke freely about her life and job at the Tampa casino. By the second glass of wine I'd almost given up on detective work. Then a photo on the screen caught my eye.

"Wait. Go back a few."

"This one?"

"One more. That one." I had her pause on a group shot. She and Foster were at the casino with a group of friends. But they weren't who I was concerned with. There was also a man, not with them but recognizable in the background. It was Magic Max. AKA my pal Squinty. Black leather jacket. Diamond earring. Looking like a young Joe Pesci.

"When was this?"

"That was the night I met Foster. He came to the casino to celebrate his birthday."

"You were working?"

Isla nodded. "Running a game for some regulars."

"You know that guy in the background?"

"No." She focused on the image only a moment, then flipped onward.

"Hold up. When was it taken?"

"Foster's twenty-ninth."

I took the phone and flipped to the days setting, noting the date.

"You know that guy or something?"

"Or something," I muttered.

She shifted on the couch and her shoulder pressed against mine. She sighed.

When I put the phone down I found her hand on my arm. Her eyes held me hostage. With her lips slightly parted, she looked vulnerable. Hungry. She finished her wine and set the glass down.

"Do you know the stages of grief, Greyson?"

"Some."

"How would you classify the one when you just want to do whatever it takes to make you feel something? Just so you know you're still alive and not the one who died."

"They just call that living."

"Since Foster's been gone I've been so lost. Like a ghost. People see me but they pass right by. Like they're scared to even ask how I'm feeling. Afraid I'll shatter. Or they ask but it's clear they have no idea what's going on inside me. I just say I'm fine. Inside it makes me want to scream."

"No one would judge you for feeling untethered, wanting something real."

"What about you?" she asked. "Do you judge me?"

Her eyes were riveted to mine, watching, begging for the truth.

"I don't."

Her fingers tightened on my forearm, then she pushed herself forward and kissed me, pressing her mouth to mine. Hard. Then ravenously.

She grasped my shirt and rolled her leg over mine, mounting my lap. My hands went to her waist.

Her hair fell around my face and she took only a short breath before taking my face between her hands and kissing me again.

Her lips tasted like sex. My fingers tightened on her hips.

After several seconds of tantalizing ecstasy, she pulled away and transfixed me with her eyes again. Her breath came fast. "This feels alive."

She tore open my shirt and put her hands to my stomach, then ran her palms up my chest to my neck. Then her mouth was on me again. She whispered into my ear, "I know I promised you dinner, but how do you feel about skipping to dessert?"

I pushed myself to the edge of the couch and rose with effort, Isla still clinging to me, her legs twisted around my waist. My left hand cupped the tight fabric of her jean shorts, my right held her naked thigh.

The bedroom wasn't far. I knew the way. The couch was even closer. But I relaxed my grip on Isla and let her body slide down mine until her bare feet touched the floor.

She peered up at me with her hair a tangle, eyes partly concealed by those improbable lashes.

"You won't," she said.

"Not tonight."

"Because I'm a mess."

"Because how matters."

I could still taste her on my lips.

"Are you going to stay for dinner?"

"I'm going to go now, or I won't be able to make myself later."

"I never made dinner."

"I know."

I released her hand and went to the door. Isla Phillips watched me go, her knuckles pressed to her lips.

Outside, I took a deep breath as I buttoned my shirt and told myself I wasn't a fool.

Because how did matter.

And because Isla Phillips was lying to me.

13

"Be glad you don't have a body, Waldo. They're nothing but trouble."

I was almost to the on-ramp for the expressway, still putting my mind back together after my encounter with Isla. My head knew I was making the right call, but the rest of me had questions. Like why had Isla come on to me only after I'd noticed the photo of Magic Max? Was the come-on a distraction? From what? Whatever the reason, it had worked. I hadn't had the wherewithal to ask her more.

"I fear I don't understand your concerns," Waldo said. "How would your carnal activity with Mrs. Phillips impact the case? The law does not prohibit it."

"Call it personal ethics."

"You wanted to fornicate with the woman. It sounds as though she felt the same."

"Do you have to use the word fornicate? You sound like a nun." I pulled into the turn lane beneath the overpass.

"A nun with an accurate grasp of the English language?"

"Accurate, but out of touch. What's wrong with sleep with? Hook up with? We need to fit with the times."

"Incoming," Waldo said.

"That's not even close to a synonym—"

"INCOMING." The accelerator went out from under my foot, launching me back in my seat as the car rocketed forward. A blur of a vehicle flashed in my peripheral vision and something clipped the rear of the car, causing it to spin hard to the left. My hands clenched the wheel but Waldo was steering, dodging a Honda Accord in the oncoming lane. Horns blared. We careened past the Honda, tires squealing as the brakes were applied. I lurched in the seat as we came to a stop.

"Fuck," I exclaimed.

"I assumed that would be too crass and pedestrian for you," Waldo said. "I'll use 'sleep with' next time."

I scanned wildly out the windshield as I clenched the steering wheel. "No. What *was* that?"

But then I saw him. The vehicle was turning around. Navy stripe. Raised up, knobby tires. I knew that truck. Dirk P. Walls. What the hell was he doing? His brights were on. Couldn't see his face, but the truck was aimed my direction.

"Oh hell no." I switched the car to manual and stepped on the accelerator. Playing chicken with a half-ton pickup wasn't a wise move but I was pissed.

The truck lurched into motion, headed for me, but swerved hard, taking the expressway on-ramp instead. The truck roared up the incline. I shifted gears and tore after him.

The old truck couldn't outrun the Boss but he was trying.

It careened around other vehicles, using the shoulder, cutting off other drivers. Horns blared.

The Boss roared after it.

The back window of the Dodge was screened by a decal with a barracuda on it. It appeared to be swimming as the truck veered between lanes on the expressway. Saturday night meant heavy traffic. The road was packed. Dirk's truck swerved around cars at what must have been close to the truck's top speed. My speedometer read 95.

Then the lane ahead opened up.

Taillights blurred into streaks of red. The truck had to have its accelerator floored. The Boss gained on him, a predator smelling blood.

He was driving like a madman. Aggressive. Bold.

But I was better. He couldn't shake me.

I only eased off the pursuit when we hit the Gandy Bridge. He had one route for the next few miles. I didn't need to cause a pileup.

"You have an address for this asshole, Waldo?"

"There is a listing for a D. Patrick Walls on Nevada Avenue Northeast in St. Petersburg. Would you like me to plan a route?"

"That's Shore Acres. I know it. Just wanted to know where he's headed."

Wall's truck looked to be slowing down. I lost sight of the pickup as it drifted into the neighboring lane and directly into the path of a tractor trailer.

What the hell?

The big rig's brake lights flashed and it gave a blast from its horn. Then it swerved left, the trailer swinging wildly. I went right to stay clear and was just in time to see Dirk's truck get hit by the front bumper of the tractor trailer. The effect torqued the front of the pickup into the concrete barrier alongside the bridge. The lifted truck rammed through the barricade in a spectacular eruption of glass, steel and concrete.

Shit.

Brake lights went on all across the freeway. Cars swerved. I tore past the scene of the crash but braked hard and veered into the breakdown lane.

That was bad. No way anyone survived that impact. But I had to check.

Another big rig thundered past as I climbed out of the car

and raced back along the shoulder, wary of inattentive drivers that might not see the accident in time.

The pickup was in the water.

I reached the point of impact and noted the bent rebar and destroyed concrete. Pieces of the truck littered the shoulder.

The water was choppy and dark, but there was enough light to make out the truck. The windshield and driver's window had shattered and water was pouring into the cab. There appeared to be no one in the seat. Thrown clear? The rear window of the cab was still intact, and the barracuda looked at home sinking beneath the waves. In a matter of seconds, the truck vanished into the bay.

Shit. I scanned the water. No sign of a body.

The waves resumed their lapping against the pilings of the bridge.

If Dirk was somewhere in that water, there was no helping him.

Sirens cut the night, and blue-and-red lights were flashing in the distance by the time I got back to the car. Traffic slowed to a crawl behind the accident.

I climbed back into the Boss.

"Your heart rate is highly elevated," Waldo said. "Do you require medical attention?"

"No. I'm fine. Just freaked out. I want to know what the hell just happened."

Emergency vehicles appeared in the shoulder at a distance behind me. I'd just be in the way. And I had no answers for them. Not yet.

I pulled back into the driving lanes and drove on, joining the flow of cars accelerating back to St. Pete.

What on earth was he thinking?

I headed for Shore Acres.

Why would Dirk try to kill me? The bump on the nose I'd given him was hardly enough cause for revenge. I wanted to be angry but the sight of the truck sinking into the bay had left me with a pit in my gut. To be angry I'd first have to untangle the knot of apprehension growing inside me.

There were things I didn't know. And things you don't know get you killed.

The neighborhood of Shore Acres hugged the bay side of St. Petersburg and had earned itself the nickname Flood Acres for the amount of water it retained in a storm. The houses were single-story ranch homes built in the seventies and eighties. The residence of D. Patrick Walls was of similar construction featuring cinder block walls, a screened porch, and carport. Old oaks lined the street but Dirk's yard held only a trio of buccaneer palms.

I parked the Boss on the street, pulled a pair of driving gloves from the glove box, and approached the front door. The street was quiet with the exception of snippets of rock music drifting from a neighboring backyard.

After donning the gloves, I tried the bell, then the door handle. Nothing moved. No sound even. Didn't Dirk Walls have a dog? My stomach turned at the idea that it might have been in the truck.

The house had no alley, but a white vinyl gate allowed access to the side yard. The back lawn was sparse, all weeds and sand spurs. Patches of turf were torn up. Small piles of dirt sat beside the holes. Dirk's dog.

Brittle PVC patio furniture and a rusted propane grill decorated the back lanai. The back door was locked as well but neatly out of sight.

I pulled my trusty lock pick set from my pocket and set to work on the door. Fifteen seconds. I considered mentioning it to Waldo but he preferred not to acknowledge my activity when it veered outside legal boundaries.

The door swung open.

The house was quiet, but something felt off. The room I'd entered was an office. Den? Video game room? Not a bedroom. TV mounted to the wall. Desk. Game consoles. Comfy recliner.

A red light glowed from a power strip taped to the floor.

Then I heard the whimper.

The dog was in a crate in the corner. A white shepherd. Brilliant blue eyes. Its head was on its paws.

"Hey. You're a pretty one." The dog's tail gave the faintest twitch, then was still again.

Then came another whimper.

I eased my way into the hallway and noted the door to the adjacent bedroom was open. Bed was unmade but empty.

A quick glance down the hall showed a living room and galley kitchen, both unoccupied.

"Why'd you try to run me off the road tonight, Dirk?" I muttered.

I walked into the master bedroom, scanned the surfaces and peeked into a few drawers, careful to leave everything as I found it.

There was an odd smell in the air. Like burnt hair. I pushed open the bathroom door. The shower curtain rail was down and a man was slumped in the tub, his head drooping on his chest.

I stooped to get a good look at his face, but it was unmistakable.

Dirk P. Walls was dead.

And he'd been that way for hours.

14

I stared at the dead body for a long time. I wondered if Dirk Walls had plans tonight he was absent from. If so, no one had come to check on him.

From what I could tell, his assailant had surprised him opening the door to the bathroom and hit him hard. Dirk stumbled back through the curtain and landed in the bathtub.

Best guess anyway.

What he was hit with was the next question. There were no signs of trauma to his head or face, but red streaks marked his neck in a fern-like pattern.

Squatting near the edge of the tub, I tugged at the collar of his shirt and found more of the burns on his chest.

They looked electrical. Like the one on my arm.

I donned my sunglasses and hit record, capturing the scene and Dirk's wounds.

I checked his pockets and found he hadn't been robbed. Still had his wallet and phone.

The marks on him made me angry. Same weapon that I'd survived at the scene of Foster's death, only Dirk didn't have a chronometer to help absorb the shock.

Back in the den I pocketed my shades and stared at the dog in the crate. How long had it been in there?

The dog watched me with a doleful expression.

Fine. I could contaminate the scene a little more.

I closed the door to the den, opened the door to the back yard, then let the dog out of the crate. She immediately went to the interior door instead.

"I'm sorry. He's not coming back."

The dog looked at me and when I failed to open the door, she slumped to the floor and pressed her nose to the crack.

I sighed.

Encouraging the dog to go out had no effect so I gripped her collar and guided her to the back door. She finally got the message and went out to do her business.

She was a beautiful dog. Animal services would be called when they found the body but how soon would that be?

After squatting in the grass the dog got distracted, sniffing a pile of dirt near the garden shed. I whistled high and loud and that got her attention. She plodded over to me and obediently slunk back in her crate.

Dirk P. Walls still had a landline in the kitchen. I picked up the phone and pressed 911. When the dispatcher picked up, I left the receiver on the counter. Someone would check it out. They'd find him.

When I looked down, I noticed the dog had crept out of her crate and was watching me. Still doleful.

Okay fine.

The dog followed me out the way I came. I locked the back door behind us and walked out via the side yard. The white shepherd stayed on my heels. I glanced up and down the street. Saw a house on the corner with a tree fort built into the lower branches of an oak. Tire swing.

"Come on."

The dog obeyed.

I rapped on the front door. A tall, thirtyish black man answered. Friendly face. Kids squealed in the background.

"Excuse me. Found this dog running loose out here. Is it yours?"

Before the man had a chance to answer, a small face appeared around the corner. Girl of perhaps seven, hair up in pink rubber bands. She rushed to the door. "Oh what a pretty dog!"

"Sasha, stay back now," her father scolded. But the little girl was already squeezing past him. "That's a stray dog, don't touch it—"

"It has a collar. It's nice!" The little girl extended a palm which was immediately licked by the dog for her efforts.

"That's not our dog," the dad said. "Looks familiar though."

"One of your neighbors possibly?" I suggested. "Hate to take it to the pound only to find it's supposed to be on this street all along."

"The pound?" The little girl looked horrified. "Daddy, don't let him take it to the pound!"

And the rest was easy.

Dad begrudgingly agreed to take the dog off my hands.

"This is just till we find the owner," he insisted to his daughter as I walked away. But she already had her arms wrapped around the dog's neck, and its tail had begun to wag.

I walked back to the Boss and climbed in.

Waldo remained uncharacteristically quiet. No Kavinsky or Daft Punk emanated from the speakers when I started the car.

"You trying to unravel this puzzle too?" I asked the car's interior as I wound my way home.

"You're the detective. I assumed you had it solved already."

"Thanks for saving my ass tonight. Don't happen to have any video of that truck trying to ram us do you?"

"Only default video functions were enabled. The collision was not recorded."

"Keep an eye on the local news for me. I'd like to know if they fish anyone out of the bay with Dirk's truck. Something tells me they aren't going to find a body.'"

"The accident would have been difficult to survive."

"Call it a hunch. Whoever was driving, it wasn't Dirk Walls."

When I got back to my apartment, I pulled into the garage and assessed the damage to the Boss. The impact to the rear fender was unsightly and had cost me a taillight, but I'd been lucky. Thanks to Waldo, I hadn't been T-boned.

I plugged the car in and started a complete system diagnostic check on the time travel subsystems. Then I went to bed.

My neck was sore in the morning.

When I got out of bed, I stretched and shuffled out to the kitchen to load the blender. My protein fruit smoothie got me moving a little faster.

Hawk followed me down the stairs at an unhurried pace. He waited for me to open the garage and rubbed his cheek against the Boss's front bumper like it was his only goal in life. I confirmed that all of the Boss's subsystems were operational and set to work fixing the taillight. Hawk jumped onto the car, walked over it and planted himself on the trunk to supervise. I replaced the taillight bulbs but had to settle for red tape for a lens. The body work would have to wait too. I had people to see.

Back upstairs, I made myself a cup of coffee and assessed my plan of attack.

I was nearing forty-eight hours of linear time on this case with no straight line to Foster's killer.

Maybe I was slipping.

My forearm itched. I pushed up my sleeve and studied the burn mark. Found some burn cream and applied it. The pattern on my skin glistened.

It gave me pause.

I located my phone and took a photo of the burn on my arm. Then I extracted a still shot from the video I took of Dirk's body. I added both to a text message. I found the contact name in my list.

Eon Whitaker. He was a trusted confidant and a veteran of some wars mankind hadn't even dreamt up in my time. If anyone knew the answer, he would.

>>> What kind of weapon leaves this mark?

The phone synced to the tachyon pulse transmitter in my jump room and I hit send.

Despite the TPT having to relay the message to the future, the reply came back immediately.

<<< Did you see it fired?

I typed back. >>> No Blast. Invisible.

Again the reply was immediate. <<< Phantom pulse cannon. Custom tech. Don't mess with it.

I typed a last question. >>> Who sells?

When the answer came, I wasn't surprised. And I had my next destination.

15

I hated going to the future. And I hated alternate futures worse.

The latter part of the twenty-first century wasn't awful. There is a period near 2080 where things are beautiful. Fully automated cars and wireless power have done away with the need for traffic signs and power poles which people had forgotten were an eyesore. For a brief window, the world looked uncluttered and clean. But it wasn't long till the digital landscape filled the void. All the billboards and store marquees that vanished from physical space multiplied in augmented reality. Soon people were paying a fortune to have a hologram-free view of their own life.

Nowhere is the digital landscape more oppressive than Shanghai.

I'd jumped to an alternate timestream just outside of ASCOTT jurisdiction. The streets were crawling with mindpill dealers, synthetic upgrade sales bots, and trans-human prostitutes. Stella York and her surveillance van buddies would probably love a shot at this action, but on this street someone would have their van on blocks and stripped of parts inside an hour.

Plus it was raining. Nobody likes to catch bad guys in the rain.

I parked the Boss in a garage and had Waldo relocate it in time to avoid trouble.

Then I went hunting.

The name Eon gave me was Zigzag. I knew her. Supposedly the only source within a couple centuries dealing phantom pulse cannons—or PPCs. I'd brought a stack of cash, set my earbuds to translate and hoped for the best.

It seemed like every door in the city had a holographic woman out front begging me to come inside and sample Shanghai's hidden pleasures. I put on my shades, activated the holo-filters, and worked on my whistling.

Waldo ran a search on PPCs and came back with not much. Street name for the weapon was "sucker punch." Couldn't find a single image on the web.

I found the spot I was looking for. Jade trinkets cluttered up a stall out front. A toothless Chinese woman with more wrinkles than God squinted at me and held up a few women's bracelets. She apparently thought I'd look good in green.

I excused myself with an embarrassing attempt at Mandarin and pushed past her into the dingy interior of the store beyond.

Dusty boxes littered the entrance. A display case ran along one side but most of the glass panels were missing. The door at the back was steel with a black buzzer button. I pressed it.

Static crackled over a hidden speaker.

"I thought you were dead."

I couldn't spot the camera. "I'm sure I am some times."

The door unlocked.

I paused before opening it. Waldo wasn't screaming any warnings. But then again, he'd have a simpler life without me.

I pushed through.

There were enough power cables running up the stairs to charge a city. I stepped over bundles as thick as tree limbs as I ascended. The second steel door at the top of the stairs stood ajar.

I pushed through and was met with the glow of projection screens surrounding a workstation. The walls were smart surfaces. One showed a city skyline and the Port Nyongo space elevator. Another was a view looking back at earth from the moon station. A third vista was obstructed by a mountain of industrial crates stamped with military logos.

Zhang Zi sat in a chair at the center of this nexus like a spider in a web. Her black hair hung long enough to cover her shoulders. She wore ripped black jeans, black boots laced halfway up her shins, and a white tank top set off by a vinyl jacket the color of a cherry Slurpee. Her meta glasses glowed neon blue.

She had a gun pointed at me.

"Greyson fucking Travers. You come to take me on a date?"

"Heard you married a synth girl from Romeo Prime."

"Ugh. Didn't work out." She took her meta glasses off and tossed them to her workstation.

Her eyeshadow was multicolored and changed hues as she spoke. "Who told you I was here?"

"Whitaker."

She lowered the pistol. "That's one of the only names that gets you not shot."

"I'll send him a gift basket. You know where I can get one full of C4 and grenades?"

That got a smile out of her.

"Who are you hunting?"

I walked the rest of the way into the room and pulled my phone from my pocket. Zhang Zi made a quick pinching motion with her left hand and suddenly the home screen of my phone appeared from thin air between us.

"You need to beef up your security."

She'd had an upgrade. Her left hand was fully synthetic now. I wondered what else was.

She started flipping through my recent image files and immediately found the video of me getting hit with the sucker punch in Foster Phillips' home office. She made a tossing motion and the video started playing on the wall that had previously been the city skyline.

"I need to know what I'm up against here," I said.

The video showed my view as I hit the floor.

"Somebody messed you up. Surprised you're still alive to talk about it."

"You know the user?"

"He's got a mask on."

"But you know the weapon. It's one of yours."

"You think I'd be stupid enough to admit to something like that?"

The image on the wall changed and suddenly it was a video of the room we were in now, only it wasn't me standing there. It was a shot of Zhang Zi and Magic Max, AKA Squinty.

"The hell?" Zhang Zi swore and made some rapid hand gestures to try to stop the video.

"Sorry about that. Waldo gets a bit nosy. When you hacked my phone you let him into your system."

"Get him out!"

She was using both hands now and trying to shut down her systems. Every time she'd close the video it would pop up in triplicate on the other wall. Soon the moonscape was covered in a hundred copies of the video all showing her selling the weapon.

Zhang Zi sprang from her chair and raced to the power terminal on the wall, flipping the lever and plunging the room in darkness. Red emergency lighting came on from the baseboards and cast her in an eerie glow. She was breathing hard and fuming.

"It was fair play."

She fixed me with a murderous stare. "Give back whatever your bot took while I was trying to shut him down."

"Gladly. What was Magic Max planning to do with the tech you sold him?"

She flexed her synthetic hand. "He finds out I told you, he'll come for me."

"No reason I need to tell anyone if you help me out."

"Son of a . . ."

"Haven't got all day."

She put her hands to her hips. "No recording."

I pulled my shades from my face and slipped them into my pocket. "Just you and me."

She flexed her jaw, then spoke. "Max had something big going down. Some kinda heist."

"What did he want to steal?"

"I don't know. Just said he needed a weapon that wouldn't be traced back to him."

"How'd that work out?"

"You know I'm dead if you tell a soul."

"What else did you sell him?"

"Nothing."

I reached into my jacket pocket and removed the wad of cash I'd brought along. I pulled several large bills from the roll and held them up. "You sure? I came to play nice."

"Nice is more expensive."

I peeled off a few more bills and she watched. I held up the larger wad.

"Sold him some refurbished Temprovibe IIIs. Off-the-Grid stuff. No tracing." Zhang Zi snatched the bills from my hand. "Who pays in cash anymore? You find this in a tar pit?"

"Would've paid more if you hadn't made it so easy." I put the rest of the money back in my pocket. "How many Temprovibes?" Max buying portable time travel tech changed things.

"Three."

"Waldo. When Zhang Zi turns the power back on, kindly replace anything you took from her. Keep no copies."

Zhang Zi pushed the power lever into the ON position and the room came back to life.

"All files have been restored," Waldo said, his voice emanating from the speaker on my phone.

"Why are you following Max?" she asked. "He answers to dangerous people."

"Just a job." I put my shades back on. "Still want me to ask you on a date?"

Zhang Zi held up her synthetic middle finger.

"Always good to see you, Zee."

"You won't find me so easily next time. I gotta move now. I hate moving."

I made my way to the door and stepped into the hall.

When I looked back, Zhang Zi was silhouetted against a starry sky. All I could see was the jacket and a faint reflection in her eyes.

"But next weekend I got no plans."

I smiled.

Then I shut the door.

The trip back to the car was wet and miserable. Waldo's small victory was the only thing keeping me warm.

"Hacking Zigzag's implant might have been extreme, buddy. Did you actually have anything on her?"

"It took an exhaustive attack to find the video I displayed," Waldo replied. "I only found it because she hadn't purged it from the security camera's active files."

"Nice bluff then."

"You *should* get her to upgrade your security. She's good at what she does."

"If she hadn't had time to wipe the file from the camera, it must have been recent. How long ago?"

"According to the video time stamp, Magic Max purchased the Temprovibes less than twenty-four hours ago."

"Wonder if one was for Tommy the Tank. We still don't know who the third is for."

"I look forward to you participating in the investigation when you get time."

"You're a riot."

The rain picked up, started coming down in sheets. Some kind of monsoon band. I ducked under an awning and tried to shake the water from my coat. People with glowing umbrellas dashed for cover as the wind blew the rain sideways.

"You're letting the cold in." The voice was in Chinese but instantly translated to English in my earpiece. I turned and found a door cracked open behind me, a golden glow coming from its edges. I took a step toward it, noting the flickering of firelight. Warmth too.

I eased the door open and took in the scene.

She was pouring hot water over a plump ceramic mug, steam wafting up and giving the air the inviting scent of lemon and ginger. A second cup was already waiting. She wore leggings that accented her womanly figure, with thick fuzzy socks. Her knitted sweater was three sizes too big for her, the sleeves bunching around her wrists and the collar hanging loose over one bare shoulder. Her brown hair was long but messily tied back revealing a slender neck and petite ears. She wore glasses and cradled her mug of tea with both hands, warming herself.

The room throbbed with heat. Out the far wall of windows was a view of heavy snow, still softly falling, piling up in drifts against the glass. The interior was hard wood and one wall was lined with a floor-to-ceiling bookshelf stacked with dusty hardbacks and dog-eared paperbacks. The room had an underlying smell of cedar.

"Don't you want to get out of those wet clothes?" She was watching me over the rim of her glasses, her impertinent lips slightly parted as she intermittently blew steam from her mug of tea.

"It looks good," I admitted.

"So do you." Her voice wasn't translated from Chinese this time. She had spoken in English.

She came closer. The sweater was soft, something made to look like angora. She filled it out with a body that left curves to explore. She put her warmed hand out and pressed it beneath the folds of my jacket.

"You're soaked through. We need to get you under the covers and heat you up. You can tell me all about your day." The bed did look inviting; a plush comforter, a half dozen pillows and an extra quilt for good measure.

Her hand trailed down my chest till she could slip it under my shirt, press it to my abdomen. So warm. She looked up at me with wide, innocent eyes. "I finished the best book today. I can't wait to tell you about it."

Her irises were an intoxicating green, deep and dazzling. She rose up on tiptoes, one hand pressed to the side of my neck, then reached for the door with the other. She began to close it.

I stopped it with the toe of my shoe.

The woman looked down, puzzled.

"You're good. I'll give you that," I said. "Sometimes I think you synths know more about what it feels like to be human than we do."

She traced my stubbled jaw with her fingertips. "Don't we all just want something real?"

"This isn't real."

"Well . . ." She smiled. "I did finish the book today. Technically."

"And a thousand others?"

The wall of windows with the snow view faded away, returning to the default smart screen logos. The bookshelves and fireplace disappeared too, replaced with clean gray walls and a heater vent. The scents still lingered. Cedar. Lemon. Ginger tea.

"You could have at least been dry." The extra pillows and quilt on the bed were gone, leaving only a rumpled bedspread with a few real pillows in plain white pillowcases.

I noted the ID on the door, pulled my phone from my pocket, keyed a number into it and authorized a small transaction.

The synth cocked her head in curiosity.

"It was a good fantasy," I said. "And you got me out of the rain."

She pressed her fingers to her lips, kissed them gently, then held them out and pressed them to mine. "Next time."

I stepped out into the cold night and took a look at the unrelenting sky. I shivered, buttoned my jacket the rest of the way up, and walked on.

The Boss showed back up in the garage on time and I climbed in, still dripping. I cranked the heater.

"Would you like me to plan a return route to 2019?" Waldo asked.

"Not yet. As long as I'm in the neighborhood, there's one more place I want to visit. And don't tell me it's a bad idea. I already know."

16

The house looked cozy. A prairie style home with enormous windows tucked between sprawling oaks. I'd climbed those limbs a thousand times as a child, chasing after my sister or as a means of spying on the neighbors. The yard was tidy, and the grass green, though the gutters needed cleaning. There was a swing on the porch.

It didn't look like the home of a family of time travelers. It looked normal. That was the idea, Mom said. To give us a simple childhood.

It wasn't raining here, though the sky held a few clouds that threatened.

Lights were on in the house. A yellow glow emanated from the floor-to-ceiling windows. Figures moved across the light. I caught Dad carrying a drink out to someone in the family room.

Parked on the street I had a clear view. Only twilight. No one had thought to close the blinds just yet.

I recognized the car in the driveway. An old Ford Galaxie. No way it was street legal here, but its owner had his way of getting around rules like that. It was no more a standard car than the

Boss was. And Grandpa Harry wasn't just some old man having a drink with his family.

But you could believe it from where I sat. A pretty picture. Simple. Was it a holiday? I hadn't thought so, but who could tell. They could be celebrating any number of things inside. Dates were just numbers in boxes, but they could choose which to occupy.

Smoke wafted from the chimney. I could smell something else too. Something cooking. That was Mom's language now. Feed people. Keep them safe. She'd done it our whole lives. Was there a person in the world better suited for it? She'd been born adrift in time, no place to call home and also a thousand places. Walked the Great Wall as it was built. Watched the colonists land at Jamestown. Visited with kings and queens of old. Became a legend in her own right. She found a place. Made a home. Expressed her love with old wine and fresh bread.

Then there she was, next to my father. The sun he orbited. Her blonde hair had darkened some over the years. A few streaks of gray. But still the center of our little universe.

She'd kept it all together, defined a future. This was it.

There was a lesson there somewhere. A woman who had the world at her fingertips, able to press pause.

Someone else passed the window. Piper. My sister, three years my elder. She was in conversation with someone in the family room.

She looked out.

The Boss was a shadow inside a shadow but she had eyes like an eagle.

A moment later my phone buzzed.

<<< You coming in?

I stared at the message. A simple enough question.

An invitation.

It seemed easy. Climb out of the car, walk the worn brick path through the yard. No need to knock. Walk right in. Hugs all around. How've you been? Great to see you.

Sit. Eat. Pretend this was all normal.

My fingers hovered over the door handle. I had just decided to climb out when another figure passed in front of the window. Tall, sandy brown hair. His face as familiar as my reflection.

It was me.

Another me.

A me that had made different choices.

The one who hadn't fucked it all up.

My hand slipped down the door frame, settled back to the steering wheel.

Just like that, the spell was broken.

Because life as a time traveler is never simple. Never clean. It's a mess of alternate timelines and paths not taken. Pandora's box. Once the lid is sprung, the contents never go back inside.

That face in the window was the proof. This wasn't my life anymore.

My sister's message still glowed on my phone. I licked my dry lips and typed a reply.

>>> Don't mention I was here.

I could see her typing as I restarted the car.

<<< Take care of yourself Grey.

I kept the headlights off until I reached the corner, the house fading in the rear-view. I tightened my grip on the wheel and shifted gears.

I needed a drink.

Waldo spoke from the audio system. "I don't think I understand your behavior, Greyson Travers."

"Don't try," I muttered.

"As you wish. Where would you like to go next?"

"Back to work. We've got a case to solve."

Waldo displayed a 3D map of time on the dash screen. "In my

estimation, there are several destinations that might prove informative. Shall I list the available options?"

"No. I'm done beating around the bush. Let's go talk to Foster Phillips."

17

Mastry's bar endures.

Dozens of other nightclubs and retro speakeasies have come and gone beside the dive bar on Central Avenue. Their high priced cocktails came in copper mugs with fancy garnishes but they weren't steeped in St. Pete history. Mastry's served cheap drinks in cheap glasses. There was a photo on the wall of Babe Ruth drinking at the original location across the street, opened in 1935, and there were guys on stools who had been drinking on the same stools since the '80s.

They finally made the smokers step outside after 2014 but the place still smells like nicotine. It was fused into the furniture with the history—soaked into the old bricks and the ancient Coca Cola logo painted on the wall.

I showed up on a Tuesday in early October of 2018 and drank cheap beer with the salty old men till after dark. I came back every other afternoon for two weeks, varying my hours only slightly. After seven days I knew each of the barflies by name and by the second week several swore they loved me like a brother. The bartenders appreciated that I wasn't pushy and left generous tips. I ducked out each night before the college kids filled the place.

With the help of time travel, I did two week's worth of drinking in only two days of my time. The hangovers were brutal but I'd managed fewer of them. It was on my third day—day fourteen in calendar time—that I finally met Foster Phillips. He came in early in the afternoon, while I was still on my first Red Stripe and sat himself a stool away from me at the bar. Jake, the bartender, had his drink poured before he asked for it. Yuengling.

"Where you been, Foster?" Jake asked.

"Working my ass off."

"Like hell. You?"

Foster flipped him the bird but Jake only smiled.

Foster caught me watching him. Eyed me warily. "You got something to say, chief?"

"This here is Alan," Jake said, nodding toward me. "Been coming in for a few weeks. He's a writer."

"Non-fiction," I said.

"How to drink at shitty bars?" Foster asked.

"Hey now." Jake's voice betrayed no real hurt.

Not like he owned the place.

I sipped my beer and eyed the hockey game on TV. The Tampa Bay Lightning were still two years away from their next Stanley Cup. But at the moment they were winning.

Foster took a drink and turned to me. "Write anything I ever heard of?"

"Probably. But not with my name on it. I'm a ghostwriter."

"What's the matter? Your own life too dull?"

"I like getting paid up front. What's your story? Maybe I'll write it."

"My story's just getting started."

"Big plans?" I asked.

He paused his beer on the way to his mouth. "Bigger than you can fit in a book."

Jake the bartender wandered back over. "Foster here already won the lottery, you ask me. Got himself the prettiest wife in town. Why don't you bring her in more, Foster?"

"And have you trying to snake her away from me? Fat chance. She's working tonight anyway."

"Tell her to put me into one of those big money games of hers," Jake said. "I could retire off one of those pots."

Foster's lip twitched at that. He looked like he wanted to say something but took a drink instead.

I took the opening. "Your girl works the tables? Casino dealer?"

"Organizer," he said. "Not a dealer. She picks the clients, sets the games. The high stakes tables reserved for celebrities."

"Any celebrities I know?"

"I could tell you all kinds of names. But I won't."

"What's your line?" I asked.

Foster took another swig of his beer. "Whatever needs doing."

"Sounds like you have it all figured out. When's this big deal of yours going down?"

"Day after none of your business. But I'll tell you this. This time next week I'll be having a margarita somewhere with an ocean view. Won't miss this place in the slightest."

This time next week he'd be dead of a hole in his head. But I thought it rude to mention it.

I paid my bar tab and rose. "Good meeting ya, buddy. Best of luck with that ocean view."

Foster nodded and went back to his beer. Bartender gave me a nod. I walked across the street and climbed into the Boss to think. In a few days Foster was going to have a gun put to his temple. I had to agree with Isla that he was too ambitious to have done it himself.

So my money was on Magic Max.

Zhang Zi had admitted she'd sold him a Temprovibe III. That meant that his being outside Foster's house the day he died wasn't any more of an alibi than it was for me. He could easily have jumped back in time same as I had.

Something Isla said came back to me. I synced my phone with the tachyon pulse transmitter at my place. I sent her a text.

>>>What was the date of the break-in at your house? The one after Foster died?

The tachyon pulse transmitter relayed the message forward in time to the date I'd selected.

It was five minutes till I got the reply with the date and estimated time. Close. A few weeks from where I was parked.

I started the car.

Waldo navigated us to the time Isla had sent. I parked down the street and watched this past Isla leave for a late shift at the Casino. I waited. It was just after midnight when the Mercedes G-Class SUV rolled by. They did a lap of the block and parked not more than a hundred yards from me. After a few minutes Max climbed out of the passenger side. He wore a beanie on his head that I was certain would roll down to cover his face as a balaclava. No gun visible but it could be under his coat. Gloves on both hands. One would be concealing the weapon that he shocked me with.

Things were starting to come together. The reason I never saw anyone go in or out of the house the day Foster died was because that wasn't when the killer entered. Max broke into the Phillips' house now, weeks after Foster was dead, in order to throw off suspicion. He jumped back in time to kill Foster, then ran into me investigating the scene from farther in the future.

It was frustrating to not be able to get out and accost him now. But I couldn't stop what had already happened from happening.

Slouched in the darkness of the Boss's interior, all I could do was think. It was looking like Max was Foster's killer, but I still didn't have a motive.

Max vanished into the backyard of the Phillips' house. The sound of a breaking window wouldn't be audible from here.

Nor would Foster's death because that was happening weeks ago.

It took only a matter of minutes until Max reemerged from the house. He glanced up and down the street, pulling the balaclava from his face as he walked to the corner. The black SUV pulled up the side street to meet him. He climbed in, then it turned my way.

I slouched lower in the seat.

"Waldo. Blackout mode."

The windshield went completely dark. The tint was so heavy I could barely make out anything outside, just the faint glow of headlights. They were slowing.

Shit.

"Exterior cameras."

I slipped my sunglasses on. Waldo projected the view of the street into my glasses, creating an augmented reality and allowing me to view the exterior as if I was seated inside a transparent bubble.

Tommy the Tank was in the driver's seat of the SUV and he studied the Boss as he went by. His eyes narrowed. Then he accelerated away, the tires on the Mercedes chirping as he took the next corner.

I told myself it was nothing. Could be he just thought it was a cool car.

No way they could know it was me inside.

Shit.

Not even I believed that. They were time travelers too. They'd be back for another look. I started the car again and pulled away, heading the opposite direction from where I saw them turn.

"First safe jump space you can find, Waldo. We gotta get out of here."

"Telephone pole on the next block makes a suitable anchor via a tether cord," Waldo said. "We'll be gone inside of sixty seconds."

I watched the rear-view mirror and tried not to hold my breath the entire minute. I breathed easier once we'd made the jump back to early 2019. My present.

"That was too close, Waldo. Whatever these guys are up to, the last thing we need is to have them gunning for us."

"Would you like me to drive from here?"

"Yep." I released my grip on the steering wheel and ran my hands through my hair. Some days I hated time travel.

I pushed my palms into my eyes and worked on clearing my head as Waldo took us back to the office. A dark cloud was looming over St. Petersburg as we crossed the Howard Frankland Bridge. By the time we reached Central Avenue the windshield was flecked with rain.

"Do I have any messages?"

"I'm having difficulty linking with the office," Waldo said as he parked the car.

"Connection issue?"

"I should have received an update from my presence in this time as soon as we got in range. I've received nothing."

I shrugged into my jacket before getting out of the car, then flipped up my collar to keep the rain off my neck as I jumped the growing puddle at the curb. The fingerprint lock on the door beeped as I was admitted. I took the stairs slowly, pulling my Stinger out of its holster as I climbed.

When I reached the landing on the second floor, nothing looked amiss, but when I tried the door to my office lobby, I found it had been pried open. I pushed on the door and it swung wide. Stuffing from the lobby chairs littered the floor. The windows that partitioned the lobby from my private office had been smashed to pieces and I could see directly into the interior.

I opened the door to my office and found it a wreck. The mini fridge was hanging open and all of the cans of beer had been poured out on the floor. The ficus was kicked over, spilling potting soil across the hardwood. So was my trash can and recycling bin. My office chairs had no stuffing so they'd been spared the gutting their lobby compatriots had endured, but someone had carved a message across the entirety of my wooden desk with what must have been a very large knife.

WHERE'S OUR MONEY?

Wow.

Hell if I knew.

Staring at the words, I had the urge to carve WHAT MONEY? underneath the scrawl, in the off chance whoever had done this planned to keep up this dialogue. Maybe I could add my phone number to avoid additional furniture damage.

But that was my mind going.

I was a detective. I should be able to figure out what money they were talking about.

Too bad I hadn't the foggiest idea.

18

"Why do they think I have their money, Waldo?"

Waldo didn't answer. Likely because I didn't have my earbuds in and the speaker in the lamp on the desk had been ripped apart. It was more of a rhetorical question anyway.

I sat in my swivel chair and took in the destroyed interior of my office. This was a mess. I opened a few drawers in the desk and found them all in disarray. It took me a minute to think through what could be missing. Foster's phone? No. This was Sunday afternoon and I'd given that back to Isla last night. I didn't keep much in the way of petty cash or anything valuable. I rummaged around but didn't note anything that was missing. This was about sending a message. I reread the carving on my desk.

Where's our money?

I didn't have anyone's money. So who did? Foster?

Foster had been dead for months.

Somebody had tried to run me off the road yesterday. Trashed my office today. Why now?

For that matter, why had Isla hired me now? Why not later? Or sooner.

I fidgeted with the settings on my chronometer. The knobs and buttons around the bezel activated a series of rings and indicators at the interior. Besides serving the function of selecting the time for a jump, it was also pleasant to watch. All these tiny movements like a well-choreographed dance.

The message on the desk was clear enough. Even if I were to back out of this case and say I was done, someone else thought I was involved—that I had their money. Or that I knew where it was.

What money?

Looking around my destroyed office, the clutter was too much. I couldn't think here. At least not here and now.

I checked my chronometer again and set it for the wee hours of Saturday morning, the first night of this. Just after I'd ridden away in Dirk Wall's truck.

Putting my fingers to the desk to ground myself in time, I jumped.

The cold beer was where I left it. Still three-quarters full. The office was tidy. No carving on the desk.

Better.

Picking up the beer, I pulled up the blinds, then took a seat in the office chair again.

Stars were peeking through the broken clouds in the sky overhead.

I propped my feet on the windowsill and thought about all I knew so far.

A widow with suspicions.

Two dead bodies.

Two thugs hanging around the scene, one of whom was almost certainly Foster's killer.

If this missing money was the issue, I had a motive. But if Foster had the missing money, why kill him before finding out where it was? Same for Dirk P. Walls. If either man had the missing cash, wouldn't they have said so to avoid death?

Magic Max and Tommy the Tank weren't Rhodes Scholars but they were smart enough to know the basic order of events for getting info out of someone.

The puzzle still had too many pieces loose. I was missing something crucial.

I sipped the beer and listened to the sounds in the street. Young people going about their Friday night oblivious of the rest of the multiverse and unaware of me or my problems. Right about now Dirk would be dropping the earlier me off in a Burger King parking lot and I'd make the long walk home to my apartment. What was it Dirk had said in the truck? Foster had something big coming up. Something to do with the casino.

I swiveled in my chair and retrieved Foster's phone from the desk drawer. Flipped to his calendar. Checked the date. It was this coming Sunday. The same date I had just come from. The note said WORK TRIP.

But Foster was dead. He wasn't going anywhere.

Unless he already had.

I shot upright in my chair, nearly spilling the remainder of my beer.

Zigzag sold Magic Max three Temprovibes. Three.

I stood, downed the rest of the beer and tossed the empty bottle into the recycling container. I'd just have to do it again when they trashed my office on Sunday but whatever. Sometimes you have to save the planet twice.

"Waldo, schedule a data backup. Save and store anything valuable off-site, then do a purge of all our on-site files before Sunday. This place is going to get trashed. Don't tell me about it when you see me between now and then, but plan for it."

"You don't wish to deter the hooligans who defile our place of business?"

"What's done is done. But I wouldn't mind getting them on video. Make sure the surveillance is running. I'll see you Sunday."

. . .

I've never been a big risk taker. The life of a time traveler comes with enough thrills. It's why games of chance never held much interest for me. But I get the allure. Watching ten dollars turn into a hundred feels like magic. An electric jolt to the pleasure centers of the brain. Hit me again.

Nowhere was that rush more on display than at the blackjack tables at the Seminole Hard Rock Casino in Tampa.

I had jumped back to Sunday night, what passed for the present day for me. I'd changed at the apartment on the way. Blazer and wingtips again. Nothing fancy but sufficient to mingle unnoticed.

The lights sparkled.

Like most casinos the interior was ostentatious: glossy marble, garish carpets in reds and golds. An Elvis Presley quote adorned an overhang near the escalators. "I just can't miss with a good luck charm like you."

The building was lit in that timeless twilight casinos use to obscure the passing hours.

I cruised the poker tables but saw no sign of Isla Phillips. I pulled out my phone and sent her a message. It was only a few minutes till my pocket vibrated with her reply. I pulled my phone back out and read her message. Then I headed for the elevator.

The main floors of the casino were busy. When I got off the elevator at the top floor, I was met with silence. I discovered it was because I still hadn't reached my destination. The elevator had reached its apex, but there was still another level to go. The private elevator up to the penthouse levels required a keycard and was manned by a burly dude in a suit that looked two sizes too small for his muscles.

I walked up and gave him a nod. "I'm a guest of Isla Phillips."

"Gotta have the password."

I flashed him the coded image Isla had texted me.

He scanned it and pulled a keycard from his wallet and opened the elevator doors for me. "Good luck tonight, sir."

I rode up to the next floor. When the doors opened, I knew I was underdressed.

The crowd was a mix of men and women in elegant evening wear. Jewels glittered on women's wrists and necks. There was a hint of cigar smoke coming from the terrace. No tuxedos, but men wore suits that may as well have been made of money.

I recognized a few faces—not personally, but from TV. Several pro athletes. One local television personality. The ones I didn't recognize were no doubt equally wealthy.

Isla Phillips made them all look like paupers. She wore a soft pink cocktail dress with a high floral- patterned neck. Cutouts in the vaguely Japanese floral design revealed hints of her naturally bronze skin. She noticed me walk in from beyond the pair of poker tables. She was in conversation with someone but gestured toward the bar with a tilt of her head. I got the message.

A woman at the bar appraised me with a predatory gaze as I walked up. She was tall, not young, but impossible to call old either. Her porcelain skin was ageless in the way very expensive things are. Her hair was extended, her breasts defied gravity, and only the skin of her hands gave any indication that she might be mortal. She wore glittering rings on both hands but none on one particular finger. She glided closer, her fingers wrapped around the stem of a coupe glass.

"You don't belong here," she said, though the words didn't come off as an accusation. They had a tone of curiosity.

"Just visiting."

"Then you need a guide." She extended her hand. "Silvie."

"Alan. I'm charmed." I held her extended fingers and brushed her knuckles with a kiss.

She shivered. "Are you the lucky kind of charmed? Be my savior. I've been losing all night." She pressed herself to my side, entwining her arm through mine.

"What are you drinking?" I asked.

"Everything."

I gestured to the bartender. He took a look at the woman on my arm and immediately started mixing her a cocktail. He handed her what looked to be a dirty martini and turned to me. "What'll it be?"

I ordered a dark and stormy. He said he had to call it something else on the bill on account of him not carrying Gosling's rum and they had a trademark on the name. I said I didn't care what he called it if it tasted good.

It did.

My lady companion was still dangling from my elbow. Seemed she didn't want to release her grip in case I up and vanished. More likely than she knew.

I kept an eye on Isla while making small talk with Silvie. She was a corporate lawyer. Killer in the courtroom. Her words. She hated the job but secretly loved the reputation. Not so secretly if she was telling me, but I wasn't going to judge.

What did I do? Oh, a writer. She had an idea for a book. Her memoir. She said I should write it for her. She'd split the profits with me.

I steered the conversation back to the room we were in. High stakes poker. She pointed out all the players she knew, described the waiting list to get in. Had to know someone. Who? Oh don't worry about that. I knew her now, wasn't that enough?

After fifteen minutes Isla broke away from the games and made her way over. She dazzled in that cocktail dress, a fact not missed by Silvie.

"Aren't you just a fantasy come to life," Silvie said, extending a hand to Isla. "You look divine, my dear."

"Always good to see you, Ms. Goldberg. Your dress is gorgeous too."

"You must go, darling. I found this mouth-watering young man wandering around unattended. He needs my full attention."

"Thanks for the invitation," I said, bowing slightly to Isla.

"He's a writer," Silvie crooned. "Isn't that just adorable?"

"I came as a guest of Mrs. Phillips tonight," I explained, separating myself from Silvie's grasp. "I'd like to have a quick word with her."

"Oh, all right. But don't forget to come back to me. We have so much to discuss."

Isla guided me toward the far end of the bar, slipping her arm around mine. She kept her voice low. "I can't usually let in any outside guests but your message sounded urgent. Is there a development?"

"Something occurred to me. Is there an object that you use here that you take home with you? Something solid that makes the trip back and forth from your house to this room?"

"Like my purse?"

"That's too variable. Something that's always the same. Rigid. Big enough that a few people could have a hand on it at once."

She glanced toward a table near the far wall. "The only other thing would be my laptop. I use it to keep track of buy-ins and the cash coming and going."

"People play with cash?"

"Not usually. It's mostly online transfers, but every once in a while we have cash games. Some of our players like to avoid the red tape with big transfers."

"What about tonight? Is tonight a cash night?"

Isla nodded slowly. "But it's kept in the safe, I'm the only one with the access code while it's here."

"Last night when we looked through photos. One was of a short guy with an earring. You said you didn't know him, but you'd seen him before."

Isla looked pained. "Only once. It was after hours. I'd had a bad night, lost some customers. He kept hounding me."

"What did he want?"

"He asked me to get him into a game here. Said he had cash and wanted to play. But I had a bad feeling when he showed up. I told him no. He got angry. But Foster arrived. Told him to clear off."

"He met Foster. He knew he was your husband?"

"Does that matter?"

"You need to get out of here."

"Why? No one can get in without—"

But she was interrupted by a scream.

19

Three men in masks had appeared from thin air in the corner of the room. Small, medium, gigantic. All of them armed. All were wearing ski masks that covered their faces but I knew who I was looking at.

Tommy the Tank couldn't blend in anywhere outside of a professional wrestler convention. Magic Max was just as squinty with a mask on. The third guy was wearing the same Tampa Bay Lightning jersey he'd been wearing the night he died. Foster Phillips. They'd used Isla's laptop as their anchor.

I hated being right. I was now looking at the last few hours of Foster's life, displaced by nearly six months.

Tommy the Tank let loose a burst of rifle fire from the weapon he was holding.

More screams. Patrons hit the deck.

I ducked too. One arm around Isla, shielding her. Her face was bloodless.

"Nobody moves and nobody gets hurt," Max shouted. They swept through the room, fanning out and performing a search. Max was carrying something big in a case. Some kind of machine roughly the size of a suitcase. It looked familiar.

Tommy the Tank locked the main doors and stood guard. Foster was the one who spotted me and Isla. Her eyes widened as he approached. She must have recognized the jersey too. It would be memorable. I felt her tense in my grip.

Foster's eyes showed a hint of recognition when he noticed me.

"Hands off her."

He pointed a gun at my face. I put my hands up.

Foster pulled Isla to her feet with his free hand and she nearly fell into him. "Come on. Take us to the safe."

The shock was evident on Isla's face. His voice. Foster alive. Her mind had to be reeling. Her mouth moved but no sound came out.

Foster glanced back at me once but then dragged Isla toward the wall nearest us.

Tommy the Tank and his semi-automatic rifle kept the rest of the patrons in place while Magic Max joined Foster and Isla at the safe in the wall.

"Get that open!" Max shouted.

She entered the combination with a shaking hand. A key code and a fingerprint scan. The safe opened with a hiss of pressurized air. Then she sank to the floor, eyes locked on Foster.

I didn't have a clear view of the contents of the box, but I saw what Max was up to. He opened the suitcase sized contraption on the floor and I recognized what it was. It was a relocation machine. Part gravitizer, part time machine. The same technology I used to jump the Boss forward and backward in time to avoid parking tickets. Only they weren't going to relocate a car.

Foster passed stacks of cash and other documents out of the safe, only pausing occasionally to check on Isla. She stayed frozen against the wall.

Max set to work running the gravitizer machine, imbuing the cash with the particles necessary to travel in time. Then he shifted them to the second half of the machine, into which he loaded a foldable storage box. He loaded the box with cash till it was full, closed the lid, entered a time sequence and hit the button. The box hummed. A moment later he opened the box again. It was empty, its contents relocated in time.

They repeated the process again and again, shoveling the money into the box. It kept vanishing.

I had to give it to them. They were going to move a mountain of cash and all they had to do was jump out of here, take the relocation machine to a safe place at the time they designated, and the money would all show back up in manageable intervals.

I considered what to do. I was close to the action but I couldn't stop them. This was their past. It had already happened. Interrupting it would only create a paradox that would do nothing but complicate this already messy situation. Max and Tommy showed no signs of recognizing me. A clue to the timeline. This was a version of them from before I met them in the SUV.

When the safe was empty, Isla snuck away from the wall, toward me.

Max closed up the relocation machine, gravitizing the storage box so it would travel again as well, but left the whole contraption on the floor. He rose and lifted his gun. "All done but the loose ends." He pointed the gun at Foster.

Well shit. That's not supposed to happen.

"No!" Isla screamed.

I was already moving. I sprung forward, launching myself toward Max. His head turned toward me, eyes wide, but he couldn't get the gun around in time. I tackled him to the floor, knocking chairs away from the nearest poker table in the process.

That was as far as my plan took me.

I was significantly bigger than Max and the tackle had knocked the wind out of him. I was hoping Foster would have the decency not to shoot me after just saving his life, but that left Tommy the Tank and his semi-automatic rifle to deal with.

I took Max's pistol away from him and peeked over the edge of the poker table. I was rewarded with a barrage of gunfire that flattened me to the floor again. Bullets shredded the top of the table and shattered the window behind me. People screamed and glass rained from the windowpane.

I covered my head. When I looked up, it was because of a shout from Tommy the Tank.

"Hey! Get away from that!"

I saw why he was yelling. Foster. He had his sleeve rolled up and the Temprovibe on his forearm was exposed. His eyes were frantic and he had his other hand on the relocation machine.

Max shouted too. If I hadn't taken his gun, I was sure he would be shooting at Foster.

As it was he had to shout to Tommy. "Kill that sonofabitch!"

But before Tommy could get his gun around to point at him, Foster activated his Temprovibe and vanished. The relocation machine went with him.

"No!" Max shouted again. He scrambled to his feet and rushed to the spot Foster had been standing.

I got to my feet as well. When Tommy the Tank turned back my way, he found me pointing Max's gun at him. His eyes widened. Would I shoot him? No. I couldn't. But he didn't know that. He dropped the rifle. But the next second his hand went to the Temprovibe on his arm. He vanished.

When I turned to where Max was standing, he had disappeared too.

The room erupted into a cacophony of shouts and screams, everyone scrambling for the exits.

I breathed a sigh of relief. But this wasn't over.

I tossed Max's gun to the top of the poker table and went to Isla. She was shaking. I took her in my arms. "It's going to be okay."

"Foster," she whispered. "That was Foster. He's alive."

"No." I replied. "Not anymore."

Sirens were sounding in the street, audible out the shattered window. I didn't want to be here when they arrived. But Isla deserved an explanation.

"When the police interview you, you can't say anything about Foster. They won't understand."

"But it was him. He was alive. The way he vanished . . ."

"Foster traveled here through time. He jumped forward to this day from a time before he died. They planned this robbery using the access he had to your laptop. It was a way in. But these guys were just using him. When he jumped back and went home, they must have found him. Killed him."

"Time travel? So he's not alive?"

"He's wearing the same clothes today. The clothes you found him in. For him this is all the same day. And it's going to end badly."

"He was right there." Isla slumped into me. I helped her to a chair, held her steady.

"I have to go. There's a chance these guys are going to come back around. Don't go home tonight. Stay with a friend. I'll call when I know more. Don't tell the police about the time travel. I promise I'll explain soon."

"Where are you going?"

"I'm going to find these guys. It's time to end this."

20

The casino was in crisis mode. I'd made it downstairs before they sealed off the penthouse levels. It was easy enough to play the role of confused bystander. The patrons downstairs had heard nothing of the gunfire but the arrival of the police had things stirred up.

Still, I made it to the parking garage without incident.

I suspected they may have the exits sealed soon so I'd have to hurry.

"Waldo, open the trunk for me, will you?"

The trunk of the Boss popped open and the interior light came on. I took off my jacket and donned my shoulder holster, making sure my Stinger was secure. But when I went to don my jacket again, my earpiece fell out and landed on the ground. I heard Waldo say something through it but it was too faint to make out. I finished adjusting my jacket, then bent down to pick up the earpiece. "What are you saying, buddy?"

But the shadow that fell over me made me turn at the same time. I looked up just in time to see the gigantic meaty fist that hit me in the face. My head ricocheted off the roof of the car. Then the lights went out.

. . .

When I came to, I was bound in the back of some kind of cargo van. Smelled like dirty laundry. Probably because it was full of dirty laundry. A towel bearing the logo of the casino hotel had been tucked under my head and when I groaned and tried to rise, I found the towel was stained with my blood.

I could feel my pulse in my scalp.

"About time you woke up, you piece of shit." Someone kicked me. I blinked and looked up to find Magic Max seated on an overturned five-gallon bucket of bleach.

The back door of the van was ajar. Parked somewhere dark, though Tommy the Tank blocked the view. I made out the sound of cicadas and frogs beyond him. Not much else. Wherever we were, it was remote. That didn't bode well for my longevity.

"Where's our fucking money?" Max punctuated the question with another kick to my gut.

I groaned. "No idea."

Magic Max gave a chuckle. "You know I should have recognized you sooner. The night you were outside Foster's place. The dog catcher. Only it was dark and I didn't give a shit." He was holding a chrome 44 Magnum Desert Eagle. He gestured with it. "But when I saw you inside the house? Then I remembered. Mister hero from the casino. Guess that sucker punch didn't make you dead as I thought it would. Going to have to use something more reliable this time."

My wrists were handcuffed behind me. I still had a chronometer on but no way to see or activate it. Not a lot of options. I squirmed but couldn't move much. "What makes you think I have your money?"

"'Cause you were in the house, weren't you. Foster walks in, he's got the relocator. I go in to get it from him, and surprise surprise he ain't got it no more. But who do I see? Mister Casino hero. Just standing there. So where is it?"

"You saw me leave when you shot me with the sucker punch. You know I don't have it."

"We done some research on you, Greyson Travers, private detective. Now I don't care what your angle is. You knockin' boots with Foster's old lady or whatever, I don't give a shit. I'm not losing no sleep over him being dead neither. But you've got money don't belong to you and now it's time to pay up."

My brain was fuzzy. He wasn't making sense.

"I didn't take the money."

"Well it wasn't in the house, so where the hell is it?" Max pressed the Desert Eagle to my temple. "You tryin' to tell me you roll up in there and pop our boy Foster and you don't do nothin' with the box? It was in that house."

I blinked.

"Hold up. You think *I* killed Foster?"

"Took me by surprise, I don't mind saying. Seeing how you pulled that hero act trying to keep *me* from shooting him. But I figure that's for the benefit of the widow, huh? Make her think you ain't the one who got rid of him."

What? My head was pounding. Maybe I hadn't heard him right.

"So . . . you're saying you didn't kill Foster," I muttered.

"How could I kill him after you killed him? You think I go around putting extra holes in dead guys for the fun of it?" He gestured with the gun again.

My head was spinning and not just from the blood loss.

I'd been wrong. I'd been so wrong.

"You didn't kill Foster," I repeated. "You were just there to find the money."

"And if you don't got it, then I guess we got no more use for you. Tommy, get this piece of shit out of here."

Tommy the Tank grabbed my ankles and dragged me backward out of the van till my feet hit the ground. He hauled me upright and held me still as Magic Max climbed out.

He wasn't Foster's killer. How had I been so blind?

Max lifted his chin. "You know why they call me Magic Max?"

"Because you make people disappear," I said.

"Because I make people—" He glared at me. "Yeah, that's right, asshole. I make chumps like you disappear."

I shrugged. "You didn't think I'd get that? You're a mafia legbreaker. Not a hard leap. Maybe they should call you Captain Obvious."

"Okay, wise guy. How you like this?" He threw a punch that snapped my head to the side. But I was expecting it. Too much arm and not enough body in the swing. Nothing like Tommy's punch. I blinked a few times and was over the worst of it.

"Tommy, take this piece of shit over to the ditch and shoot his ass."

"Why I gotta do it?" Tommy moaned. "I like this gun."

"Then you should be excited to use it."

"'Cause then I gotta chuck it in the river. I'm tired of throwing my shit in the river. Maybe this time I use your gun and we throw that in the river."

"My gun? My gun is brand new. On account of this asshole taking my last one." Magic Max drew the chromed Desert Eagle from his shoulder holster. "This is a thing of beauty right here. Not throwing my gun in the river. You nuts?"

"Then why didn't you bring another gun? I'm not throwing mine in the river neither."

"If I might offer a suggestion," I said. "You can use my gun. I won't be needing it after."

Magic Max stared at me, then at Tommy the Tank. "So use his fucking gun." He gestured toward me. "You need the marks to tell you how to do your job now?"

Tommy shrugged and walked to the passenger door of the van. He came back with my shoulder rig, hung it on the open rear door of the van and pulled my Stinger 1911 from the molded holster. In his hand it looked small. He lumbered back to me and waved the gun. "Okay, let's go."

I walked past the van and toward the bend in the road ahead. We were still a dozen yards from the guardrail when he called to me. "That's far enough."

I kept going but looked back over my shoulder. "Not going to tell you how to do your job the way your partner does, but if we go up around the corner a little there's more shrubbery and such. I fall down the ditch here some biker will see it right away. Up there? Hell, that'll take 'em days to find a body and you won't even have to drag me down the hill. Probably roll right into that scrub brush."

Tommy peered toward the far end of the guardrail.

"Plus, if you pop me here, Max'll think you're lazy. Then you'll have to drag me. I ate a heavy lunch."

"Just shut your mouth for once and keep walking."

By the time we reached the far side of the guardrail, we were just out of range of the car's headlights. I walked to the edge of the shoulder. I wasn't wrong. If I rolled down this hill and wasn't already dead, the fall would kill me. It was steep enough that someone would have to be looking almost straight down to notice a body.

I turned around to face Tommy the Tank. He was breathing heavily from the walk but trying not to show it.

"You stick around a while, maybe you add some cardio to your day."

"Shut up." He leveled my Stinger at my head. "You got any last words?"

"You have my phone? I want you to record them."

"What?"

"My last words. I need you to record them for me on my phone. You just push the red button on the camera app."

"I know how to record a video."

"Okay, so do it. You can show it to your boss later to prove you shot me."

He begrudgingly fished in his pockets for my phone and opened the camera. He held it up. "Okay, what's this important message?"

I looked directly into the camera. "I'm ready, Waldo."

Tommy the Tank's eyebrows furrowed. "You're a weird dude, you know that?" He tossed my phone to the ground, pointed the gun at my face and squeezed the trigger.

Nothing happened.

"The hell?" he muttered and checked the gun. He popped the magazine out and back in again and chambered another round. The previous round ejected onto the asphalt and hit with a ping.

He pointed the gun at my face again and squeezed.

Nothing.

"What kind of piece of shit gun is this?"

"One not made in the dark ages," I said.

While he was still focused on the gun, I took two quick steps forward and kicked him hard in the groin. "Mother fu. . ." he managed as he doubled over. Then he finally went for his own gun. I backpedaled, angling sideways to the very edge of the road. He dropped the Stinger and switched his Ruger to his dominant hand. He almost had it aimed when a black shadow erupted from the darkness and the front end of the Boss caught him mid thigh. Tommy the Tank rolled partway up the hood before the car braked hard and he was launched forward amid a squeal of rubber. Tommy's lower body clipped the edge of the guardrail before cartwheeling over the edge of the ravine. He hit the slope of the hillside at least once on the way down, but by the time I got myself to the edge to look over, he was sprawled at the bottom of the slope with his neck broken and legs splayed out at an odd angle.

I turned back to the car. "Thanks buddy. Electric drive system comes in handy, huh?" Waldo flashed the running lights once in response. I scooted around to the passenger side of the car, pried the door open and managed to access the glove box by backing into the car butt first. I located my lock pick set in the glove box. I had a few spare handcuff keys floating around but opted for a shim instead, sliding the thin strip of metal between the pawl of one locking mechanism, then the other.

Ten seconds. Not my fastest time but now wasn't the occasion to mope about it. I walked around the front of the car again and Waldo backed the Boss up, revealing my Stinger on the ground where Tommy the Tank had dropped it.

It unlocked in my hand the instant I picked it up. I also retrieved my phone.

Magic Max had to be wondering what had become of us by now and as I strode a few yards back around the bend, he was just visible in the passenger side of the cargo van. The door was open and the dome light was on, limiting his night vision and lighting him up like the target he was. I caught faint snippets of rock music. I raised my gun and kept it aimed at his head as I walked. I was still forty yards away. He hadn't looked up. Thirty-five yards.

He must have sensed something. He turned the van radio down, squinted even more than usual. Should have his eyes checked.

Thirty yards. I only had nine rounds in the Stinger. He had cover. Patience. He climbed out of the passenger seat. "Tommy, what the hell is taking so—"

I squeezed the trigger. The shot was low and left but caught the edge of his trapezius muscle between his neck and right shoulder. He shrieked and ducked behind the door as my second shot went where his head had just been.

A vehicle door could stop a round from this distance so I waited him out. A moment later his hand appeared with a pistol in it. He squeezed off a few rounds, spraying wildly and nothing coming close. The gun was a cannon but he couldn't see anything.

A roar erupted behind me as the gas engine on the Boss came to life. The car's tires squealed as it tore from its position behind me and flew past. Magic Max peeked his head up over the window frame just in time to see the car coming. He shrieked again and dove into the interior of the van just before the Boss's front bumper clipped the passenger door and slammed it onto whatever part of Max was still sticking out. My guess was a foot.

He howled.

Waldo took the Boss past the van, then torqued into an aggressive one-eighty, the rear tires sliding over the damp pavement. The car ended in an angry posture, front tires turned and headlights illuminating the van.

The top of Max's head appeared in the vicinity of the steering wheel and I squeezed off another shot. The bullet passed through the windshield and tore apart the seat cushion but missed his head.

He shouted from the interior. "Don't shoot! We can work this out!" He'd somehow managed to scramble into the driver's seat. The ignition turned over.

I took careful aim and shot out the right front tire.

Max tried to drive off anyway but Waldo was there. He used the bumper of the Boss to nudge the rear fender of the van. Combined with the blown front tire, it was enough to make the van careen into the guardrail.

Max fell out of the passenger side of the van and tried to make a run for it but the engine on the Boss snarled. Waldo gave every impression he was going to run him over.

"Drop the gun!" I shouted.

Max turned with his hands up and tossed the pistol away. The collar of his shirt was soaked with blood.

"You won't see me no more, you hear me? You let me go, you'll never see me again."

"I don't believe you. The only reason I'm keeping you alive is that I need you to deliver a message. Tell Roman Amadeus that I'm going to find that money but he won't see a cent of it. It'll go right back to the casino where it belongs. Here on out, you stay out of my way and I'll stay out of yours. We'll call it square. You understand?"

Max narrowed his eyes. "Back to the casino? You ain't gonna keep it?"

I shook my head.

"I can live with that," Max said. He lowered his arms.

"Get the hell out of here."

He reached slowly for his shirt sleeve, rolled it up and entered something on the keypad of his Temprovibe. He gave me one last leering grin and vanished.

I lowered my gun and groaned my way over to the Boss.

My face hurt.

Climbing inside, I took the time to belt myself into the five-point harness. "Looks like I owe you another one, Waldo."

"Does this mean I'm getting a raise?"

"I wasn't aware I was paying you. Figured you did all this out of the goodness of your heart."

"I have no heart."

"More than some I've known."

"Would you like to go home?"

I stared out the windshield at the battered laundry van. "This isn't over yet. Max didn't kill Foster Phillips."

"If Max wasn't the killer, the logical assumption would be that Foster Phillips did commit suicide."

The starry black sky outside seemed to be taunting me with its vast expanse of nothingness. "It doesn't feel right."

"Are you concerned about telling Mrs. Phillips you were wrong?"

"No. I just can't shake the feeling there's something I'm missing."

"You think your feelings are something of value?"

"Just do me a favor and pull up the images from my sunglasses cam at Foster's time of death."

Waldo displayed the video on the dash. It started playing. My scan of the room. Magic Max showing up, blasting me with the sucker punch. Me hitting the floor.

I played it again.

The scene unfolded once more. Foster seated at his tidy desk. A loose pen cap. Where was the pen? Computer open. The hole in his head. Gun on the floor. Max came in, shot me. I hit the ground.

Played it again. This time when the scene opened to the shot of Foster at his empty desk I sat up so fast the seat harness caught me.

"Are you all right, sir?" Waldo asked.

"It wasn't something I was missing, Waldo. It's something that *was* missing."

I stepped on the clutch and reached for the gear shifter.

"You have a destination in mind?"

"Damn right I do. Because I just solved this case."

21

I hadn't been to Puerto Vallarta in years. The Pacific Ocean was turquoise today, and the beach crowded. Tourists roamed the sand, walked the corkscrew pier or scuttled about in rental boats. I had another destination.

The vacation condo sat off the main strip, away from the high-rise condos. Real estate sites said it belonged to a wealthy couple from Winnipeg named Otto and June. They hadn't been there lately, but the rental schedule online showed that their place had been occupied for nearly six months.

I parked the Boss in a dusty turnabout and studied the exterior of the bungalow for several minutes before walking partway up the curved drive. The front of the house faced the distant view of the water over the brim of an infinity pool. I took a circuitous route through the neighbor's yard and emerged in the bungalow's backyard. The lawn was patchy and poorly watered. The only blemish on an otherwise good-looking house.

I preset a jump time on my chronometer before walking up to the bungalow. Just in case.

The sliding back door was open and only a screen obstructed the entrance. It wasn't locked.

I slid the screen open quietly and stepped inside, scanning the kitchen. A spacious living room extended from the opposite side of a bar, and a wall of windows looked out toward the pacific. A cool breeze was blowing from offshore and made everything smell of salt, but there was another smell inside. A peeled orange had been split open and left on the counter, a few segments missing. There was an open beer near it, three-quarters full.

The ceiling fan hummed.

I walked through the kitchen into the living area, noting the dated glass coffee table and oak entertainment center that said Otto and June hadn't redecorated in over a decade. With a view like this, no one would be focused on the furniture.

I was watching whitecaps rise and fall on the turquoise water when someone chambered a round in a gun behind me. My guess was a Glock.

I held my open hands out to show I was unarmed.

"You got some kind of nerve walking in here." The male voice was even and calm. "Any reason I shouldn't end you right now?"

"Because ghosts don't kill people . . . Foster."

I turned slowly to face the man with the gun.

Foster Phillips was wearing a linen shirt and Bermuda shorts. His hair was damp. I guessed he'd been in the pool not long ago. His clear blue eyes focused on my face. "How'd you find me?"

"Dogged persistence."

Foster gave a snort. "What gave me away?"

I shrugged. "Not too many corpses around who pen their suicide notes *after* they're dead."

"You were one of the guys who barged in and snooped around the house."

I slowly lowered my hands to my sides. "Convenient that there were two of us. Max and I had each other pegged as your killer for much longer than we should have. I figure you must still have been in the house too. Master bedroom maybe?"

"Couldn't think straight to write the note looking at my own dead body. Too weird."

"Have to hand it to you. Pretty clever coming up with that idea on the fly. Or did you have it planned the whole time?"

"Nah. Really thought about ending it."

"So you sat in that chair contemplating killing yourself and then what? Remembered you still had a time machine?"

"Remembered I had another way out."

"So you went into the other room, jumped back in time a few minutes, then walked back into the office and blew yourself away before you even had the idea. Swapped the guns, went back into the bedroom, wrote the note, hid out from me and Max while we blundered around, and I'm guessing you were gone before Isla got home. Or did you stay to watch? To see her face when she found you."

"I didn't need to see that. I didn't do it to hurt her."

"You certainly stumped the police. Handwriting analysis matched. Only your fingerprints on the gun and the note. Max and I were the only ones who could've seen there was no note on the desk at the time of your death. It was a nearly perfect murder."

"It wasn't murder. I'm still here. Only I'm free."

"What about Dirk Walls? He's the piece of the puzzle I'm still not clear on. Did he know you were alive?"

Foster swallowed. Lowered the gun slightly. "I went to his place after I did it. Told him to keep an eye on Isla for me. Didn't want her running off while I was gone. I had to wait till after the casino job to come back for her or it would have screwed up the timeline. I was going to pay him more from the take when I got back."

"But Max and Tank found him first."

"Damn fool must have spent some of the money I gave him at the casino while he was watching Isla. That's the only way they could have known he was in on it. By the time I got back to his place they'd killed him."

"He didn't know showing up with gravitized cash would have him flagged as being connected to a time traveler."

"I didn't think to warn him. When I found out, it was too late."

"Wasn't the only thing you screwed up."

Foster scowled. "How so?"

"You left a grieving widow who was distraught enough to hire a determined private detective."

"So distraught she had to sleep with a private detective you mean? I saw you together, the night before I would've come back for her. I saw you through the window."

"Ah. Figured you might be the one who tried to run me off the road. Time traveling out of Dirk's truck before the crash was a nice touch. But I didn't sleep with your wife that night. And you were dead."

"My body was barely cold."

"Seemed that way to you maybe. Months for her. But you figured you'd leave her in the lurch? Like she had it coming?"

"Are you kidding? I did all of this for her! And she betrayed me. I saw you with your arm around her at the casino, didn't want to believe it, but then seeing you through the window only confirmed it."

"You don't see how backwards you have it."

His hand had drooped with the weight of the gun as we spoke but he snapped it upright again. "You mocking me?"

"I get that your mind wasn't right after your team turned on you. The stress of the heist. What was the deal? I'm guessing Max propositioned you when Isla wouldn't let him into the cash poker games."

"Never planned it to go this way. I only went along to make sure she didn't get hurt. These guys would have eventually found a way in there with or without me."

"But this way appealed to your big plans. You thought you'd

grab Isla and go on the run with the cash. But then you saw her cheating on you."

"She never could stay single. Not once in her life. I should've known."

I rolled my eyes. "You don't deserve her."

"You know what? Go to hell." His finger came off the trigger guard at the same time my hand found the chronometer pin on my other wrist. I caught the first hint of the muzzle flash the instant I vanished.

It was pitch black in the house.

I'd chosen three o'clock in the morning as my arrival time. It's the time with the highest probability of nothing moving in a house.

There certainly was nothing moving in this one.

I took a deep breath and walked toward the space Foster had been standing and positioned myself just to one side, out of the line of fire from his pistol but close enough for what I had planned. I flexed both arms, shook them out, then took a nicely balanced stance before raising my chronometer to catch the dim light of the moon off the pacific. I set it for half a second after I'd left and pushed the pin.

Gunsmoke filled my nostrils as soon as I arrived. I'd missed the bang, but not the aftermath. The bullet from the gun punched through the front window and made its way toward the Pacific. My fist took Foster Phillips in the side of the jaw.

Punch through your target. That's the key.

He went down at an angle, his body colliding with one of the barstools on the way down. He hit the floor hard.

I shook out my fingers and checked the results of my work. Foster wasn't knocked out but he was dazed. I'd seen the look plenty. The gun had fallen from his fingers so I picked it up and tossed it onto the counter.

"As I was saying, you're an idiot for not realizing what you had. Isla was distraught. Grieving. Needed comfort. She didn't betray you. Being lonely isn't easy."

He still seemed dazed, but when he looked up, I got the impression my words had registered.

"Maybe you should try consulting your wife *before* you run off to Mexico. I hear communication is the key to a happy marriage."

I took my phone from my pocket and pulled up my contacts. I fired off a quick message.

By the time I'd finished, Foster was looking more alert.

"Here's what's going to happen," I said. "In a minute, a bunch of Time Crimes agents are going to bust in here and arrest you. You're going to do some time for theft and abuse of temporal machinery. Probably less time if you're willing to cooperate and spill whatever you know on Magic Max and his buddies. Good news is it's time travel jail so when you get out they'll put you back anywhere you like. You can pick up where you left off with Isla, assuming she'll still have you. I recommend your first words to her start with 'I'm sorry.'"

Foster climbed slowly off the floor and I gestured toward a bar stool. He took it.

"I almost killed you," he muttered. "And now you're giving me marriage advice?"

"Tried to kill me. Let's not give you too much credit." I pocketed my phone. "And it turns out I'm a romantic. Who knew."

22

I was sitting in a rocking chair on the front porch of the vacation rental enjoying the cool tropical breeze when Agent Stella York finally made her way over. Time Crimes agents had Foster loaded in a transport carrier and would be hauling him off to Rookwood Penitentiary to await his trial. The prison for criminal time travelers was located in the mid twenty-second century. Inmates liked to call it 'Time Out.'

Stella studied me, then tucked her hands into her bomber jacket as she leaned against the porch railing. "Playa Los Muertos, huh?"

"He told his friend there was a beach for the dead. Turns out he was being literal."

"Seems like Foster will play ball. Says he's willing to give us everything he knows on Magic Max and Tommy the Tank."

"Tommy is dead. You'll find him stinking up a ditch. I can give you the coordinates."

"Your handiwork?" She arched an eyebrow.

"Tragic car accident. Had nothing to do with it."

"Hmm. Convenient. You're willing to verify that?"

"Only because you asked so nicely. What's Foster looking at for charges?"

"He might get lucky. I don't know if it was intentional, but he offed himself so quickly, and did such a good job getting out of town, the local timeline never split. I doubt it even gave anyone a headache. ASCOTT can't charge him with creating more than a ten-minute localized paradox. He'll have to own up to his involvement in the casino theft, but he wasn't the mastermind behind the heist. They'll want to go after bigger fish."

"You have a way to put Foster back into linear society again after he does his time?"

"That'll be tough. Hard to explain to a guy's friends how he came back from the dead. But maybe the wife will be willing to relocate. We can place them in an alternate timeline with a clean start for his probation."

"You found the money?"

"Back bedroom. That temporal relocation machine went missing from an ASCOTT stockpile a century from now. We're grateful to recover it. Money will go back to the Tampa casino. You won't be happy about the next bit of news I have for you though."

"No finder's fee?"

"The casino is owned in part by Roman Amadeus."

I furrowed my brow. "Amadeus' thugs were stealing from his own casino?"

"Turns out the casino had recently taken out an extensive anti-theft insurance policy. Linear people of course. They would have had no chance of ever discovering the stolen cash once it was relocated in time."

"So Roman would have made insurance money from stealing his own cash. Now we have to give it back. At worst he's back where he started. Can you pin the fraud on him?"

Stella shrugged. "Doubtful. I suspect it was all part of the larger strategy of laundering mob money through the casino but we can't prove it. We picked up Magic Max in a neighboring timeline trying to trade in his black market Temprovibe. He's going to testify that the whole heist was Tommy the Tank's idea. Amadeus never knew anything about it."

"Of course he is."

"That's the way these things go. Amadeus will make a mistake one of these days. If we caught all the bad guys we'd both be out of a job."

"Doesn't sound like the worst option."

Stella stared out at the Pacific. "Vacations are overrated."

"Maybe you and I should stay a few days and try it out. Just to see what the fuss is about."

She turned and appraised me with a shake of her head. "Nice try. Work friends stay at work."

"Oh, so we're friends now?"

"I'm not arresting you yet. That's something."

I propped my feet on the porch railing. "Every relationship needs room to grow."

Stella shook her head again, this time with a laugh. She stepped off the porch and walked away to rejoin her fellow agents. I didn't mind the view. Because even from this angle, I could tell she was smiling.

23

Monday morning I was sitting in my office staring at the clock. The cleaning service had done its job. The mess was gone and a repairman had refinished the top of my desk. He was now working on cleaning the new lobby windows.

Isla Phillips walked up the stairs at 10:57 and came into my office without knocking.

I stood.

She wore an off-the-shoulder sweater dress in storm-cloud gray. High boots obscured her legs from the knee down but the near scandalous hemline of the sweater dress left the majority of her thighs bare. She walked in and set her pocketbook on the edge of my desk, then took a seat without speaking a word.

I sat again.

We stared at each other. Her from behind voluminous lashes.

"I didn't hear from you last night but I decided to come in today as you suggested. I was beginning to think I was going crazy."

"When you came into my office on Friday, I made you a promise," I said. "That if you showed up at eleven this morning, I'd give you the truth. I'm afraid I've broken that promise."

Isla glanced at the clock. It was a minute past eleven.

"You can't imagine I'd fault you a matter of sixty seconds. Are you saying you can't give me the truth? If you need more time—"

"I don't."

She pursed her lips. "Is it because of how I came on to you the other night? You want to be rid of me? I'd had a lot to drink and—"

"Mrs. Phillips, however complicated our involvement the other night turned out, it wouldn't have kept me from telling you the truth. This is something more complex than that." I entwined my fingers on my lap. "The resolution is going to be complicated too. In a few days you're going to be contacted by an agency in possession of Foster Phillips."

"His body? It's been cremated."

"His person. It turns out your husband went to elaborate means to fake his death."

Isla Phillips locked eyes with me. Confusion changing to anger. "I'm the one that found him. I washed his blood from my—" her lips quivered as she tried to get the words out. "You told me—"

"I know the situation is inconceivable. But I was wrong before. Your husband *is* alive."

She glared at me, reading my face. "Why? Why would he do such a horrible thing?"

"Escape. To get clear of the trouble he'd gotten you into. And because he underestimated the means you'd employ to avenge him."

"Avenge." Her voice was flat but somewhere in the word was a question.

"Me. He saw us together the other night. He thought you'd betrayed him."

She wilted. "He did?"

"When you see him again I suspect he'll feel differently."

"You spoke to Foster."

"And you will too. Soon."

"And the men who wanted him dead?"

"They won't be bothering you anymore."

"How long have you known he was alive? Before Saturday night?"

"I didn't suspect it then. That wasn't why I didn't stay."

"You thought I was broken."

"No. But I know I am."

Her expression changed—her brow furrowed. "No. This is absurd. First you tell me it's time travel. Now you say Foster is alive? You have any proof? You said yourself there's something you're not telling me."

"I'm not telling you how it works."

"You can't or won't?"

"The agency who has Foster wants to be the one to explain it to you. Help you adjust."

"Then how do I know you're telling me the truth about the rest?"

"It will become evident. In time. Foster has always been striving for a way out. He never got free, not really, but this will be your chance. When these people call—and they will—pick up. Whether you take Foster back after what he did is up to you. But either way, it'll be a fresh start. A real one."

Isla twisted the wedding ring on her finger, then stood. "I owe you the rest of your money."

"Use it to start your new life."

"But you earned it."

"Didn't do it for the money. Let me be generous this time."

She bit her lip. Then nodded.

I stood and walked her to the door, opened it for her.

She stepped close and still smelled of summer. But it was a summer I couldn't know.

Isla paused next to me, placed one hand on my shoulder, rose to her tiptoes and kissed the corner of my mouth, lingered there. Then she whispered "Thank you" and walked out.

I closed the door slower than usual.

Walking back to my chair, I put my hands in my pockets and stared out the window.

Waldo's voice emanated from the speaker in the lamp. "My job as your assistant would be easier if you collected the full fee for our services. We do have bills to pay."

"I'll make it up on the next one."

Out the window, Isla Phillips climbed into her white Volvo and was lost to view.

"Do you think they'll work it out? Mr. and Mrs. Phillips?" Waldo asked.

"Hard to say. Predicting the future isn't in my job description. I just work there."

"Speaking of which, would you like me to cue the next of your cases? Someone has just walked into one of your future offices. They insist on seeing you. It seems someone they care about has gone missing."

"Which office?"

"Port Nyongo. In 2099."

I pulled myself away from the window and ran a hand through my hair. "Sure. About time for a change of scenery anyway." I adjusted the dials on my wrist. "Double-check my coordinates for me?"

"Your settings are perfect, as always."

I pressed my hand to the edge of the desk. "You know what? Why don't you bring the car."

Waldo's voice had a hint of excitement to it this time. "We'll meet you there, sir."

I smiled. Then I donned my sunglasses, pressed the pin on my chronometer, and vanished into the future.

Thanks for reading *Time of Death!* Greyson's adventures will continue. Want to know more about our time traveling detective?

For a look at the days leading up to this story, download three exclusive bonus chapters, including how Greyson ended up with the Boss. Get your bonus here.

https://BookHip.com/LWPZAX

Then read on for a sample of *Clockwise and Gone*, a free time travel thriller that takes place in the same world.

-NVC

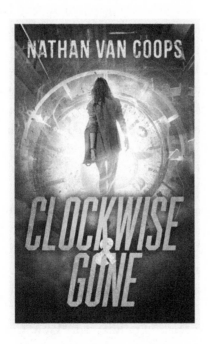

Chapter 1

"To your promotion," Dom said, raising the glass of champagne. "New head of Gammatech's Safety Division."

Emily reached for her nearly-empty glass and held it aloft gently. "Thanks to you."

"I had hardly anything to do with it." Dom snatched the bottle from the bucket of ice and quickly topped off her champagne flute. "Management at Gammatech just knows a winner when they see one." He grinned and clinked his glass against hers. "You earned it."

Emily smiled and took a sip. She certainly had done everything in her power to prove herself at the energy company but that hadn't stopped the rumors and muttering behind her back—the whispers that she was only where she was because she had slept her way to the top. Dom laughed off the idea that anyone would doubt her resume, but no one had ever said anything to him directly. He was Dominic Del Toro, son of the owner of the company. He was immune.

Emily was not.

She had no doubt that there would be sideways glances on Monday when she was back at the office, but she was determined to enjoy the champagne anyway. She took another sip and took in the expansive view of the illuminated city skyline. She would enjoy tonight. Monday's problems could wait.

The server's reflection in the glass made her turn her gaze back to the bustling restaurant.

"Can I interest you in any dessert this evening?" He cleared away her plate and handed it off to a passing busboy.

"I actually hoped we could have the special tonight, Felipe. The one I called ahead about?" Dom said.

"Of course, sir." Felipe smiled. "I'll get that for you right away."

"Call-ahead special?" Emily asked. "Wow. Courtside seats at the game, now specialty desserts— you really did go all out tonight."

"Well, not quite yet," Dom said. He slid out of his seat and reached into his pocket as he stood. "There was one more thing I was hoping to discuss. One question that wasn't in your interview from the board yesterday."

Emily stared at the small black box in his hand. He was getting on one knee. Oh wow, this was happening now?

"Emily Marie Davis, from the first time I saw you, I was completely and utterly in love with you. Even all the way back at uni when you wouldn't give me the time of day." Dom smiled at her. "I would do absolutely anything to keep you in my life forever. Would you do me the honor of marrying me?"

Emily stared at the sparkling diamond as he opened the box, and realized her hand was shaking when some champagne sloshed onto the table. She hastily set the glass down.

"Oh my God. I can't believe you are doing this." Marriage. This was really happening.

He grinned up at her. "So, what do you say? Would you like to be Mrs. Del Toro?"

Emily looked into his eager eyes and slid out of her chair. Her breath seemed caught inside her, but finally she got the words out. "Yes, of course. Yes."

He stood to wrap his arms around her and she pressed her lips to his. Over the thrumming of her heartbeat in her ears, she registered the clapping and cheering of the other diners in the restaurant. But just barely. They may as well have been in another world.

The elevator ride to the street was a blur. She didn't even remember leaving the restaurant. There had been a dessert. A cake? She vaguely recalled that much. Another bottle of champagne had been opened too. That was still with them. Dom carried the half empty bottle with him to the car. As his vehicle pulled to the curb they climbed into the back laughing.

"Home, Avery," Dom managed, before Emily tackled him and started planting kisses all over his face.

"Proceeding to Regency Tower." The car's automated

response system flashed the destination on a screen and engaged its drive motor.

Emily stopped kissing Dom long enough to admire the ring on her finger again. He'd really outdone himself this time.

"You like it?" Dom studied her with eager eyes.

"I love it. It's beautiful."

"Still doesn't compare to you," Dom replied.

As Emily reached for him again, the car's speaker came on and the voice of Dom's life management system, Avery, spoke. "A call coming in for you, sir. Inspector Walsh from subsection Delta."

"I'm a little busy right now," Dom replied between Emily's smothering kisses.

"He's all mine tonight, Avery," Emily said.

"The call is marked urgent," Avery replied. "How would you like me to respond?"

"Inspectors always think everything is urgent," Dom said. "Tell him I'll call him back."

"Yes, sir," Avery replied.

The car arrived at Regency Tower entirely too quickly as far as Emily was concerned. She had barely gotten Dom's tie off him, let alone anything else. He was altogether too buttoned up for her taste.

They were engaged. She had a fiance. It had seemed like a made-up word till now.

She let it roll around her mind as she carried her shoes and let Dom lead her toward the elevator. Her head was decidedly fuzzy from the champagne, but something about the ring on her finger was making him irresistible tonight. She entwined her fingers through his and leaned her head onto his shoulder in the elevator. He was wearing the cologne she'd gotten him for Christmas. She took a deep breath. Yes. This was going to be a good night.

Dom wasn't the most physically attractive man she had ever

dated. If you had asked her yesterday she might even have said he wasn't in the top five. He lacked the height and athleticism she usually looked for. She had always dated ball players in college. Dom's physique was far better suited for a golf course than a basketball court. His jump shot was atrocious. He worked out when he could, but as heir to the Gammatech empire, he spent far more time in board meetings than at the gym. Add in the receding hairline, and Dom might even be considered homely by some. But what he lacked in looks he had more than made up for in devotion.

Ever since she moved back to the city, he'd been pursuing her. No. Longer than that. She could remember him trying to walk her home from parties in college, back before he'd lost his glasses. He'd always had style, and women interested in his money certainly fawned over him, but he used to show up to her games in a suit and tie. Not at all what she was looking for then. He'd even visited her in the hospital the night she tore her ACL and ended her dreams of going pro. Despite his continued attention, she'd barely given him a second glance. During the years since college she rarely thought of him at all unless it was at Christmas or her birthday. He always remembered to send a card. Real mail. Hardly anyone did that anymore.

Those were the little things that added up in the end.

When she finished with her energy contracts abroad and decided to search for a job back in the states, it was Dom that had contacted her immediately. He said he'd seen her resume and thought she'd be a wonderful fit at Gammatech. A management track with a salary that made competitor's offers look laughable. How could she say no?

The doors dinged open at the penthouse. His penthouse. Would they live here after they were married? The thought gave her pause. This was all happening so fast.

"Avery, please set lights to level 2," Dom said as they entered.

The normally bright lighting dimmed to a soft glow.

"Are you feeling okay?" Dom asked, smiling at her. Emily realized she was still latched to his arm and slowly unwrapped herself.

"Yes. But I think I need more champagne. You'll go find us some?"

Dom brushed a strand of her hair behind her ear. "I'm already as elated as I've ever been. More booze won't help."

Emily grabbed his hand and kissed his fingers. "Yes, but I need a minute to get sexy for you."

"You're already sexy," Dom grinned.

"Champagne," Emily commanded, pointing toward the kitchen. "Your fiancee says she needs champagne!"

He let go of her fingers and bowed, then turned toward the kitchen.

She did not need more champagne.

Her head was already swimming, but she was going to do this right. She pushed through the door to his bedroom and dropped her shoes near the closet doors. She should have planned ahead better. If she had known this was coming she would have tried to stash something here to wear. Something other than the yoga pants and old sweatshirt she kept stuffed in the bottom drawer of his dresser for nights she slept over. That wasn't going to cut it tonight.

She considered just stripping bare on the bed and waiting, but shook off the thought. She was feeling far too full from dinner to be up for that. She would opt for one of his button-down shirts. It wasn't lingerie, but he'd still like it. Can't beat the classics.

A cork popped from somewhere in the vicinity of the living room.

She ditched her dress on the floor and walked to the bathroom mirror to determine the appropriate amount of buttons to employ on the shirt. Once there she took a look at the state of her wavy chestnut hair and frowned. She was trying to get it back into some semblance of a style when Avery chimed from the other room.

"Call from Inspector Danvers, marked as urgent."

"Danvers?" Dom asked. "From Sector Echo?"

"Yes. There are also three other inspectors on the line. They've requested you join a community call. Shall I engage a video conference?"

"No!" Emily shouted from the bathroom. "He's busy."

"No video," Dom said as he walked into the bedroom.

"Hey, I'm not ready for you yet," Emily said. "You go there." She pointed him toward the bed.

"I might need to take this call," Dom said. "It sounds important."

"It's Saturday night. We just got engaged. Can't it wait?"

"I'm just going to see what's going on. Maybe it's nothing."

Avery chimed in. "Mr. Del Toro Senior has also joined the call but is requesting a private conversation."

Dom squeezed Emily's hand, then walked back into the other room.

Emily frowned and slumped onto the bed.

"Avery?"

"Yes, Miss Davis?"

"We're going to need to talk about his priorities . . ."

"I would be happy to provide any service Dom requires," Avery replied.

"I'll bet you would," Emily muttered.

She propelled herself off the bed and only wavered momentarily before pushing her way out the door to the living room.

Dom had his jacket back on and was attempting to retie his tie.

"You're leaving?" Emily said. "Where are you going?"

"I need to get down to the plant and check on things. This new shipment of control rods I ordered for the reactor is giving us some strange indications. The inspectors called a meeting. I guess it's pretty serious."

"Is everyone at the plant okay?"

"Yeah, absolutely. Just stay here. I'll be back as soon as I can." He finished the tie, then patted his jacket pockets, doing an inventory, before stepping over and kissing her. "Don't go anywhere."

"Fine," Emily said, pouting her lower lip, but adjusting his collar to better cover the tie.

He kissed her one more time, then slipped out the door. "Be back soon."

Emily stood staring at the closed door for a few seconds, then turned slowly on her heel to check her other options. The newly opened bottle of champagne was still sitting on the counter. She slouched over to it and snatched one of the glasses up before trudging back to the bedroom.

"Looks like it's just the two of us, Avery."

"Would you like to view entertainment options, Miss Davis? Perhaps the highlights from the afternoon's games?"

"Not tonight. I think I just want a bath. Will you fill the tub?"

"Bathtub will be filled in approximately eleven minutes. Would you like to choose a scent for your bath oils?"

"What does Dom use?"

"Mr. Del Toro prefers lavender and tea tree."

"Interesting. I'll try that." Emily took a sip of champagne. "And some music please." The penthouse filled with soothing instrumental piano music. "Something from this century," Emily said.

She was still bickering with Avery about the music choices when she heard the elevator ding in the hall. A moment later, footsteps sounded in the kitchen.

She opened the bedroom door and looked back out. "Dom?"

Dom had his back to her, rooting through a drawer in the kitchen, but turned around at the sound of her voice.

"That was fast," Emily said. "False alarm?"

He wasn't wearing a tie anymore. He looked ... tired. Like the few minutes he'd been gone had aged him.

"Hello, Emily," Dom said. He stared at her, looking her up and down. "You look ... well."

Well? She was half-naked in his shirt wearing a brand new engagement ring and 'well' was the best compliment he could muster?

"What happened?" she said aloud.

"We need to go," Dom replied. He strode across the room and grabbed her by the wrist.

"What? Go where?"

But he was already pulling her across the room toward the elevator.

"Dom, I can't go anywhere. I'm not dressed and it's late. I thought we were staying in. Ow. You're hurting me."

Dom's grip on her wrist was like a vice. He dragged her into the foyer. The elevator doors opened and he spun her inside.

"I don't have my shoes," Emily objected.

"You don't need them."

"Where are we going?"

He didn't reply. He was preoccupied with checking his phone. He studied the time, then shoved the phone back in his pocket. Emily stared at him but he seemed intent on ignoring her.

His face was stubbled. Hadn't he been clean shaven earlier tonight? Emily studied the shadow on his chin with confusion. How much champagne had she drunk? Things were getting strange.

The elevator reached the garage level and Dom hauled her forward across the oil-stained concrete to a waiting car. It wasn't his car, but Dom flung the door open without a moment's hesitation. "Come on. Get in."

"I want your jacket."

"What?"

"Give me your jacket. You're hauling me off to somewhere you won't explain. I'm not going in just your shirt."

"Why does it matter?" Dom asked. "We won't be seeing anyone."

Emily held out her hand for the jacket.

Dom sighed and took it off, then tossed it to her. He pushed her toward the car. Come on. We've got to go."

Emily climbed into the rear-facing bench seat and slipped her arms into the jacket. She wrapped it around herself and tucked her dirty feet up underneath her.

"Why on earth can't we just stay in the penthouse? What's the big hurry?"

Dom was glancing at his phone again. "You'll know soon enough. Avery, take us to Section Kilo."

"The research division?" Emily asked. Gammatech had what seemed like a thousand departments on a dozen campuses around the city, but she'd made a point of learning them all.

"Here. I need you to drink this." Dom held out a glass bottle of bright blue liquid. "It'll help you sober up."

"Then you drink it," Emily replied. "You're the one acting like a crazy person."

Dom shrugged, unscrewed the cap on the bottle, and took a swig. Then he held it out to her again.

Emily glared at him, but then took the bottle. Her head was beginning to throb. Hydration wasn't a bad idea. She took a sip and let the blue liquid course down her throat. It tasted like . . . What was it? Something she'd never felt. Like liquid lightning. Her throat tingled with it.

She considered Dom seated across from her. He was simply staring out the window. She sniffed and wrinkled her nose, then tried to locate the scent she was smelling. It was coming from his jacket. She lifted the collar and held it to her nose. Cologne. But one she'd never smelled before. When would he have had time to get more cologne? The bathtub hadn't even filled in the time he was gone.

She looked at her fiance across the back of the car. His expression was hard to read in the shadowy interior.

He *had* been clean shaven tonight. All those kisses.

"Dom?" she tried softly this time. "What's going on?"

When he looked at her, his eyes were serious. "You'll just have to trust me."

"But why can't you tell me what's happening? I'm getting frightened. You're freaking me out."

"Emily." He leaned forward and rested a hand on her knee. "In all the time you've known me, has there ever been anything I've done that wasn't in the interest of keeping you with me? Of keeping you safe?"

"No. Never."

"Then believe me when I tell you now. There is nothing I wouldn't do to keep you from harm."

"Are we in danger?" Emily asked.

Dom looked back out the window as the vehicle slowed. "Not for much longer. Drink the rest of that, then come on. We're here."

Chapter 2

The concrete sidewalk leading to the research facility was cold on Emily's bare feet. She shivered a little and wrapped Dom's jacket around herself a little tighter. A security guard at the entrance tipped his hat to Dom.

"Good to see you again, sir. Twice in one night." He smiled and opened the door for them.

The doorway traded cold concrete for cold epoxy flooring that was slick beneath her feet.

Dom didn't slow his pace at all as he guided her through several hallways to what must have been the back of the building. He finally stopped at a doorway that had been chained shut and padlocked. Dom entered a combination and unlocked it, then pulled the entire chain free. Emily noticed that the combination had been her birthday, 4-9-20. Dom took a glance down the hallway they came from, then pulled the door open. "Okay. Here we go."

Emily wasn't sure what she expected, but the room they walked into wasn't it. It looked like an oversized storage closet. Dusty metal racks lined the walls, home for a few outdated computers and forgotten hard drives. There was a window on the far end of the room but the opaque glass squares only let in the faintest glow from the streetlight. Dom flipped the switch and illuminated the room with harsh fluorescent light.

He ran the chain through the door handles again and refastened the lock.

"About time," someone said. "I thought you said you'd be quick."

Emily located the speaker sitting in a folding chair in the corner. He rocked forward and stood, shaking out the length of his overcoat and stomping his feet. He was skinny, dressed in all black, and smoking an electronic cigarette. She hadn't seen one of those in years.

"Why are you just lurking here in the dark?" Dom said. "It's creepy."

"You wanted me to stay here. I stayed. You didn't say you needed me awake."

Dom turned toward Emily. "This is a new acquaintance of mine. What did you say your name was again?"

"Axle."

"Well, Axle, did you at least prepare things for me like I asked you to?"

"Setup's all ready. Standard stuff." He pointed to a rolling office chair and a contraption against the wall that looked like some kind of door frame.

"Dom, what's going on?" Emily said. "You really need to tell me what we're doing here. Who is this guy?"

"We're getting away for a little," Dom said. "I've got somewhere where we can go to get things sorted out. I've got a way to keep you safe."

Emily noticed that Axle was eyeing her bare legs and tried to tug the edge of Dom's jacket a little lower.

"You don't mind me saying so, mack, you got a fine looking lady here. Lots going for you. You sure you don't want to just forget this plan and go off and enjoy her somewhere? I'm thinking I would."

"Shut your damn mouth," Dom growled at him. "I didn't pay you for your suggestions. I paid you to do your job. Just get things ready. We're wasting time."

Axle held up his hands. "Whatever you say, mack. You're the boss." He stepped over to the doorframe erected by the wall and started fiddling with a control panel attached to the side. A number of heavy-duty cables were running across the floor and were directly wired into the breaker box on the wall.

"Emily, I need to tell you something," Dom said. "I'm sorry to keep you in the dark about this but we're almost safe. There is going to be a problem at the plant. The reactor core is growing unstable. It's going to . . . It's going to do a lot of damage. But I have somewhere to take us. I can fix things. I just need you to come with me. It's all going to be okay."

"The main reactor?"

As she spoke, the door frame against the wall started buzzing. The space between the posts began to shimmer, then erupted into a field of multicolored light. The colors swirled and twisted in an eerie sort of harmony with one another. Emily found herself transfixed by their beauty.

"What is that?" she murmured.

"Our future," Dom replied. "Have a seat."

Dom wheeled a rolling office chair over and Emily sat, almost automatically, her eyes still glued to the luminescent doorway. She didn't look away until something cold closed over her wrist. She looked down to find her arm handcuffed to the chair.

"Hey, what the hell?"

"Standard procedure," Axle muttered from next to her..

"Procedure for what?" Emily demanded.

Dom shoved Axle out of the way and knelt in front of Emily. He rested a hand on her knee, then held up another bottle of blue liquid. "I need you to drink this."

"What the hell is that stuff, Dom? And don't give me that 'sober you up' bullshit."

"It's going to help stabilize your cells," Dom replied. "The more we get into you, the safer you'll be."

Axle wheeled an IV rack over to her chair and started prepping a syringe.

"You have got to be kidding," Emily replied. She snatched the bottle from his hand and threw it across the room. "I'm not drinking anything until you explain what you're doing to me."

Dom closed his eyes for a moment, then grabbed her arm and took her hand between his. "Emily." He opened his eyes again and stared into hers. "That machine over there is going to take us somewhere new. But in order to get there, we need to treat your body with a special sort of particle. It will protect you and enable you to travel safely. But only if we get enough into you to make it work."

"Why aren't you cuffed to a chair? Why isn't he?" She looked to Axle who was now wheeling some other contraption made of hollow tubing toward them.

"We've already had our treatment," Dom replied. He kissed her hand then laid her forearm against the arm of the chair. "Now I need you to stay still." He wrapped a fabric strap quickly around her arm and fastened the Velcro.

"Hey! No. Dom!" Emily tried to jerk her arm loose but it was strapped tight. She tried moving her other arm but the metal handcuffs only rattled against the chair. "I don't want to do this. Let me go!"

"There is no other way," Dom replied. He grasped her face between his hands. "Your future depends on this."

"Dom." She stared at him with her most no-nonsense expression. "I want to go home. Let. Me. Go."

But Dom simply strapped a band around her other arm and secured it tightly to the chair as well. Axle bent down with the needle.

"Get that away from me!" she shouted.

"It's going to hurt more if you move," Axle replied. He pressed on the inside of her arm, probing for her vein.

"Don't you touch me with that—" she began, but it was too late. He already started inserting the needle. She froze. When the IV was in, he taped the tube to her arm and stood up.

She caught him staring down her shirt. She jerked against the arm of the chair but it was no use. Why hadn't she used . . . more . . . buttons . . .

She felt dizzy. Her head lolled slightly.

"What else did you put in there?" Dom asked.

"Just something to calm her down. Figured we may as well get a head start on the rest of it."

Dom frowned but didn't object. He stood, and swayed with the rest of the room as it turned. It was all getting wavy.

Emily's pulse was throbbing in her ears with the rhythm of a clock but the men seemed to be moving in slow motion. She tilted her head as Axle wheeled the tubular structure overtop of her seat. It was a sort of framework, bolted together with space in the interior for her, and with what looked to be plastic sheeting around the edges. She felt like she was in a portable shower. A bright light illuminated the sheeting. It was clear, but difficult to see through. The room had been going blurry before, but now it was even more difficult to see. Dom was just a vague shape on the other side of the curtain.

"Dom?" Her voice came out softer than she intended. She meant to yell at him but it only sounded like pleading.

"Where are you—" the air crackled with static and blue light flickered around the curtain. She saw now that it wasn't plastic, but rather some sort of conductive material ribbed with fine strands of metal. Electricity danced and tingled across her skin and seemed to burn through her veins. She cried out from the shock of it.

Moments later it was over.

The two men were muttering something on the other side of the curtain, continuing to ignore her, when a loud bang erupted near the doorway. A blinding light flashed, causing her to squint and blink, and then there were voices. The overhead lights went out. Her ears were ringing. Axle shouted. Something crashed to the floor amid a scuffle ahead of her.

"Get her loose!" a man shouted.

Someone collided with the curtain and she caught a glimpse of Axle, snarling and drawing a knife from his belt. The multicolored light emanating from the strange doorway behind her was barely enough to see anything, but she felt hands on her right arm, someone unwrapping the Velcro straps.

"Dom?"

But it wasn't Dom. A face in a black ski mask appeared in front of her. They unstrapped her other arm.

"Listen, you have to run!" It was a woman's voice.

"No! Don't touch her!" Dom shouted as he flung the tubular framework aside and grabbed for the woman in the mask. She backed away and he pursued her, fist raised.

Emily tried to rise from the chair but her left arm was still handcuffed to it. She wobbled and sat back down. What had they given her?

She was about to try again, but then Axle was there, his

leering expression illuminated by the eerie flickering light. "You ain't going anywhere, honey. Except gone." He put a hand on the chair arm, and the other over her handcuffed wrist. Then he pushed her, hard, toward the multi-colored doorway. His hand ripped the IV from her arm as he shoved. "Have a nice trip!"

"No, wait!" Dom shouted.

Emily attempted to plant her feet to stop her momentum but her bare heels just slid across the slick epoxy floor. The wheels of the office chair wobbled but her trajectory was true. She rolled right into the swirl of light and color.

There was a fraction of a moment where she felt like she'd departed her body and was soaring through the cosmos.

Then the wheel of the office chair hit something and she tipped, nearly spilling out of it onto the floor. The chair teetered, then settled back onto its wheels, planting her in the seat in a room once again filled with fluorescent light. There was a medical table, some silver trays on wheels, and someone standing in front of her. She looked up to find a man in paper scrubs and latex gloves looming over her. He was wearing a paper mask and had a foot jammed against one of the chair's wheels.

"Well, what did Axle bring us today?" the man asked.

Footsteps sounded from behind her and when she spun around in the chair she found a second masked doctor on her other side. He was holding a scalpel. "Not bad looking, this time," he said. "Pity. Get her on the table. Let's open her up."

Finish this story for free!

https://dl.bookfunnel.com/997t8zzj7o

189

ACKNOWLEDGMENTS

A very special thanks to author Alan Janney (Alan Lee) who gave tremendous advice as I entered the world of mystery writing. His books and characters inspired me and got me excited to try out this genre.

Each book I write would be riddled with errors if not for the efforts of my outstanding beta team. The Type Pros gave me feedback, caught my typos and have been a source of encouragement along the path to publishing this novel. My special thanks to:

Eric Lizotte, Marilyn Bourdeau, Judy Eiler, Rick Bradley, Maarja Kruusmets, Mark Hale, Andrew Freeman, Gary Smart, Ginelle Blanch, Alissa Nesson, Felicia Rodriguez, Ken Robbins, Bethany Cousins, Claire Manger, Sarah Bush and Kay Clark.

Every book I write is better than I could ever make it because of you.

ABOUT THE AUTHOR

Nathan Van Coops lives in St. Petersburg, Florida on a diet comprised mainly of tacos. When not tinkering on old airplanes, he writes heroic adventure stories that explore imaginative new worlds. He is the author of the time travel adventure series *In Times Like These*, and *The Skylighter Adventures*. His series *Kingdom of Engines* explores a swashbuckling alternate history where the modern and medieval collide. Learn more at www.nathanvancoops.com

OTHER SERIES BY NATHAN VAN COOPS

In Times Like These

The Kingdom of Engines

The Skylighter Adventures

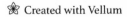

Made in the USA
Las Vegas, NV
11 April 2022

47267188R00111